THE KEEPER
OF THE WIND

By Mark A. Shaw

Printed in the United States of America

First Printing, 2014

ISBN 978-0-9936768-1-9

Lillie Publishing
#13-7273 17th Ave
Burnaby, BC V3N 1L1

Mervo1985@gmail.com
www.facebook.com/lilliepublishing
https://twitter.com/MarkTheShaw
marktheshaw.tumblr.com

Book design & Page setting by: M A D (www.mad.com.bd)

To my grandmother Lillie Smith –Your love made me the man that I am today.

And to my children-There is no love greater than what I feel for you.

Contents

PROLOGUE
The Past

During the American Indian Wars in the 1800's, a group of mystical shamans from many different tribes banded together. Through an ancient ritual, they asked the Heavens and Mother Earth for a tool to defeat the White Man, who were killing their people, raping their women and taking their land. Heading the ceremony was Mundoo, who was not only the chief of the largest tribe of the land, but also the wisest and the most powerful shaman. He was the one whom many of the other shamans of this newly formed band had apprenticed under before moving onto other tribes.

The group of shamans sat in a circular formation around a large fire and began to chant in their native tongues. As the ritual was taking place, the fire grew, taking on the forms of animals and elements of nature. All of a sudden the sky started to darken and a lightning storm followed. All the while, the shamans continued to chant and pray until suddenly, a very strong wind blew out the fire and knocked them all to the ground. Right after they were knocked to the ground, the storm and the winds stopped—all that was left within the circle and the mist was a staff, a wolf's hide, and a feathered crown. Wrapped around the staff was what seemed to be a talisman; it was oval-shaped and forged with a metal not known around that period. Connected to the metal piece was a thick cord, attached to which were wild feathers and multicolored beads. On the face of the metal was a burned in encryption in old Native writing, reading *"Only the pure of heart can be worthy."* Not knowing what powers the items possessed, the head shaman, Mundoo, gave the staff to Moki, his young apprentice. Moki, who was pure of heart, tried to wield the power within the staff. As he touched it, he felt a surge of power flow through him. He felt at one with the heavens and the earth as his body levitated from the ground for a brief moment. Everyone stood in amazement when Mongwau, the second in command, became jealous and demanded to be the one to have the staff, as he was next in line to be head shaman. This would have been true, but Mongwau had been found to be studying the forbidden dark arts in secret, and because of this he was not granted his wish. A fight had ensued between Mundoo and Mongwau, but after he was defeated Mongwau left the tribe with some of the other shamans following behind him, suspected followers of the dark arts as well.

Mongwau and the shamans who'd joined him decided they had to have the power of the staff. Mongwau and his followers went to other tribes, spreading lies that Mondoo and the other shamans had a powerful tool and were going to join the White Man to use it against the tribes so that they could split the lands and rule together. Mongwau told the tribes that he and the shamans with him could use their powers, along with tribal warriors, to defeat Mondoo and rid the lands of the White Man with the powerful tool that Mondoo and the other shamans had. Out of fear, the tribes decided to join forces with Mongwau and the other evil shamans to attack his old tribe. As the days went on, word got back to Mondoo of the lies Mongwau and the evil shamans were spreading, and that the other tribes planned on attacking them in the next two days at sunrise. As the day approached, a scout was sent to observe at sunrise. Over the horizon, he saw that thousands of warriors from other tribes descending upon them. The scout went back to Mondoo with this information. Moki, armed with only the staff, was sent in alone.

As he stood on the last hill between them and his tribe, he yelled to the warriors, "We are all one people; to fight each other is not the key to being free and keeping our lands! You have been told lies—Mongwau and his shamans are evil and only want the power for themselves!"

Mongwau yelled out that the others were the liars and urged the warriors to attack. Blinded with rage, they began to charge up the hill and toward the camp. Moki began tapping the staff on the ground and chanting the words *"wytobse n arowby,"* and with each chant got louder and louder, until suddenly the wind started to pick up and swirl around him, lifting him up from the ground. There, with his arms extended and the staff in one hand, his eyes glowed white, and for a moment, everyone froze in amazement, unsure of what to do, when Mongwau yelled, "He is the only one now – we have to attack!"

So began the charge again, ascending up the hill. Moki, realizing he could not reach their hearts or minds, spoke to them in a somber voice, "So be it!" and with a wave of his staff, he started to throw multiple tornadoes at them, sweeping them up by the hundreds and throwing the warriors miles away. Some tried throwing spears and axes at him, but none could touch Moki. Those who were not swept up by the tornadoes began running for their lives, never to attack them again. Mongwau and the two other evil shamans disappeared. Legend has it that once the good shamans saw how powerful the staff was, they feared that others would come to try and obtain its mighty power. In order to prevent it from falling into the wrong hands the staff—called Wytobse, with the power of the four winds – was hidden, never to be used again.

CHAPTER 1
The Future

It was a beautiful spring day in Seattle—the sun was out and the leaves on the trees were green again. It was an unusually warm day, where three best friends roll off the bus one by one: Tim Wilson, a Caucasian boy; Olivia Linn, a Hispanic girl; and Marcus Avery, an African-American boy. All were seventeen-year-old high school seniors attending Mervo High School, currently on a seniors' school camping trip in the Wenatchee Forest. This trip, which happened every year for the seniors at Mervo High, was the last school trip of the year. Marcus and Olivia both came from "the hood" and were bussed by their parents to the suburbs to attend school so that they would have a chance at a better education. Tim was from suburbia, a "cultured" household, but had a love for all music, and especially soul music—that was what they all had in common. The three met while playing in the school band and soon found out that their interest in music went much further than simply common ground. Olivia loved to sing and play guitar, Marcus played the piano and wrote his own music, and Tim could play guitar as well as a variety of other instruments. Sometimes, the three would go to Tim's house and jam together. Tim's parents were big music lovers as well; they, too held a love for all genres of music, and they would sometimes sit in on the jam sessions to cheer the kids on.

At the campground, Olivia mentioned to Tim and Marcus that she had heard from her brother about a freshwater lake not far from the campsite; he had gone there when he went on the same senior camping trip the previous year. He had said it was about a forty-five-minute hike east of the campsite. The three decided to go, and lied to the camp staff that they were going to look for more firewood. Once they were safely out of sight, they started heading east. They had walked almost forty-five minutes when they came upon a beautiful lake.

The three friends stopped and looked at each other with happy, silly grins as Tim hollered, "Last one in has to buy dinner when we get home!"

They all dropped their backpacks and jumped into the water fully clothed. Marcus won the bet and Tim lost, but it didn't really matter, as they were having fun.

After about an hour, they all decided to head back to the camp before anyone started to worry. As they began their hike back to the campsite, the sky started to darken and a light drizzle of rain started to fall. A few minutes later, the light drizzle turned into an all-out lighting storm. In their haste to find shelter from the weather, the three veered off the trail and got lost.

Eventually, they saw what looked like an opening on the side of the mountain and they ran to seek shelter. As they stood, drenched and trying to catch their breath, Marcus said, "Where the hell did that storm come from?"

Tim quipped, "Hey man, we got bigger problems right now—we're freakin' lost!"

"Well, I guess we will just have to ride out this storm in here, won't we?" Olivia replied as she sat down on a big rock in the corner.

Frustrated with the fact that they were stuck, Tim leaned back on what he thought was a rock wall with vines all over it, and ended up falling through into what was obviously a cave that had been covered up with vines.

"What the hell?!" Tim screamed as he fell onto his back on the ground.

Olivia was intrigued. "A cave... cool."

"I'm not going in there! There might be bears in there or something!" Marcus exclaimed.

"Oh, Marcus, stop being a punk," Olivia said, scrunching up her nose.

"Yeah, man, where's your sense of adventure?" said Tim, eyeing Marcus.

Marcus shrugged his shoulders. "Man, whatever." He turned to enter the dark, dank cave. "If I get eaten by a bear or cougar, I'll come back and haunt your dreams!" he said dryly with a crooked grin.

The cave was dark, musty, and cold, but it was still better than being out in the storm. The three sat close to the entrance of the cave. Nearly an hour had passed when they realized they were cold, wet and hungry.

Marcus smacked his lips. "A triple-patty burger with

cheese and fries would be so good right now!"

Tim jumped in. "Yeah I'm feeling a large meat-lover's extra-cheese pizza! And I would wash it down with a large iced tea!"

"Yeah, right now, I want a great big salad with a splash of lemon juice on it, and a side of baked tofu. Then wash that down with a big bottle of water!" Olivia added.

They all stopped, looked at each other, and then burst into laughter, when all of a sudden, Tim heard faint voices coming from the cave, "Hey, did y'all hear that?"

Marcus, looking a little bewildered answered, "Hear what?"

"Those voices," said Tim, almost in a whisper.

"That's probably us echoing," Marcus said, trying to be comforting.

"Yeah, the acoustics are pretty strong here, I could probably record a song." Then Olivia turned and said loudly, "Watch this...ALL THE SINGLE LADIES!"

"All the single ladies all the single ladies all the single ladies all the single ladies!"

Hearing it echo throughout, Olivia smiled. "See what I mean?"

Just after that was said, faint chanting voices started up again, and this time they all heard it, but it lasted only for a few seconds.

"What the hell! That ain't Beyoncé!" yelled Olivia.

"Hell naw, that ain't even Kelly Rowland," Marcus added.

"Now I'm getting creeped the hell out!" Olivia shuddered.

Tim shouted out, "Hello, is anybody there?" It echoed, but there was no response.

"Man, this is so weird," Marcus said, looking at Tim.

Tim started walking. "I wonder where it's coming from?" he asked as he started to go deeper into the cave to investigate.

Olivia called after him, "Tim, what the hell are you doing?"

Tim said, matter-of-factly, "I wanna know where that's coming from."

Trying to keep things light, Marcus threw his hands up. "How come in situations like this, the white guy always seems to want to know?"

"Ha ha, you got jokes—so are you urban wussies coming or not?" Tim pulled out a lighter from his pack and proceeded deeper into the cave with Olivia and Marcus nervously in tow.

"You know this goes against my blackness, right?" Marcus tapped Tim.

"Don't worry, my friend, what happens in the cave stays in the cave," said Tim, copying the Las Vegas catch-line.

"Literally." Olivia smiled, and deeper into the cave they all went.

The deeper into the cave they got, the darker it became. Olivia said, "Hey, look over there on the wall, it looks like torches!"

They all walked over to the wall to get a close-up look when Marcus said, "These are like something you'd see in an old movie. You think they still work?"

"I sure hope so, but there's only one way to find out. Grab a couple of them." Tim picked a couple up to light them, and they lit with no problem.

"Cool, this is much better," Olivia responded.

"Who you telling?" Marcus questioned.

Tim looked puzzled. "Someone's been here before; these torches didn't get here by themselves."

"Maybe somebody hid money in here, or some treasure," Olivia added.

Marcus rolled his eyes. "Yeah, and maybe Yogi and Boo Boo are sleeping up ahead." He and Olivia both laughed, but Tim remained focused and serious.

They had only walked a little further when the faint voices started up again, sounding like a chant. The three stopped and looked to their left to discover a tunnel opening. The voices seemed to be coming out of it.

"I think it's coming from in there," Olivia said as they

approached the opening.

They all hesitated for a couple of minutes at the entrance, when Tim took a deep breath and said, "Fuck it, we've come this far, let's do this!"

"Okay, you go first and we'll be behind you, like waaaayyy behind you!" Marcus replied.

Olivia agreed.

Tim chuckled, "So much for you two being from the hood. You two both just lost your street cred."

"STREET CRED? First of all, you know nothing about street cred, and secondly, look around you—we ain't on no damn street, we in some spooky-ass cave chasing ghostly voices!" said Marcus.

Olivia added, "Yeah, fo' real; what's wrong with this picture?"

"I'm pretty sure our friends back in the hood would give us a street cred pass for this one," Marcus pointed out.

Olivia jokingly replied, "True, but we won't get a stupidity pass!" She laughed.

"Whatever, losers." Tim pushed forward. "I'm going in."

"Go on then," Marcus urged.

"I am," Tim replied as he started making his way into the tunnel.

After a few minutes, Olivia turned to Marcus. "As crazy

as this is, you know we can't leave him in there alone, right?"

With a frustrated sigh, Marcus nodded. "Yeah, I know; come on, let's go." And in they went to join Tim.

They couldn't see Tim for the first few minutes into the tunnel, but Olivia saw his torchlight in the distance and knew he was up ahead.

Marcus called out to him, "Hey, Tim!"

Tim turned to see them and waved. "I knew you couldn't leave me!"

As the three started walking toward each other, the faint chanting voices started up again. This time however, it was continuous and getting louder and louder for at least several seconds before it suddenly stopped.

"It's getting louder and more intense," Marcus noted.

"I got a really bad feeling about this," Olivia replied.

Marcus agreed and yelled out to Tim, "Tim, man, let's get up out of here!"

"I'm right behind you!" Tim hollered back. Just then, the chanting became even louder, almost like shouting, and the cave started to shake as if there was an earthquake.

Marcus looked at Olivia and in a serious tone said, "Yo, I'm out!" As he started running toward the entrance of the tunnel, Olivia started running too, with Tim not even ten feet behind her. Marcus was the first to exit the tunnel, falling to the ground, with Olivia just seconds behind him. Tim was only a few seconds behind the both of them, but they raced back to the tunnel entrance and yelled for Tim to come on and hurry up.

"Does it look like I'm walking?" Tim yelled as he ran, but just before he was able to reach his friends in the main cave, the ground crumbled beneath him.

"No!" Marcus screamed as he saw Tim fall into the hole that opened up below him.

"Oh my God!" Olivia cried.

The voices stopped and the cave stopped shaking.

CHAPTER 2
The Discovery

Olivia and Marcus thought the worst seeing Tim fall into the ground. They rushed to the hole and began to shout for him, hoping against hope that he was all right. At first there was no answer, which left them both scared and panicked. They couldn't see Tim in the hole; all they could see was darkness. They tried calling him again a second and third time.

"Tim, are you okay?"

All of a sudden they heard a moan and a cough, then Olivia said, "Oh my God, Tim, are you okay?"

Tim begrudgingly replied, "Yeah, I think most of me is." Then he jokingly added, "But I think my ass is going to need surgery." Marcus and Olivia exhaled in unison, then laughed.

Then Marcus replied, "Yeah, maybe they can even put an ass there where you thought you had one." They all laughed.

"Hey funny man, can you make like MacGyver and find a way to get me outta here?" Tim asked.

"Hold on," Olivia said. She and Marcus began to search for something to pull him out of the hole with. Marcus suggested going out in the storm to grab a big tree branch to put in the hole and try to pull him up with it. Olivia agreed and they got up to leave the cave. Pushing through the wreckage of vines, Olivia suddenly got an idea.

"Marcus, if we can tie a bunch of these vines together, we can make a really strong rope to pull Tim out of that hole," she said. Marcus glanced at the vines and nodded his head.

"Sounds good to me!" he exclaimed as he started to grab at the vines. A few meters away, Tim was still stuck in darkness of the hole. He fumbled in his pocket for his lighter, which he promptly lit. He was not in a hole.

Tim began to walk around as he realized he was standing in a small dungeon-like room. He moved the lighter around the room when he suddenly screamed and jumped back, dropping it to the ground and then quickly picking it back up.

"Oh shit! I'm not the only one down here!" he screamed. Slouched against each corner of the room were four skeletons dressed in what appeared to be ancient Native attire. He could also see torches lining the walls of the room. Gathering his courage, he walked over to the torches and lit them. Now in the lighted room, Tim could now see ancient Native text written on the walls. In the middle of the room stood an altar with three items propped up on it: a wolf's hide, a crown of feathers, and what looked like an old staff.

Olivia and Marcus, who had heard Tim's scream, were peering into the lit room.

"Tim, are you all right?" Olivia yelled.

"I'm fine," Tim said. "You guys have to see this, though!

This isn't a hole—it's a room! There are four skeletons and some weird altar in here, too."

"That sounds pretty cool… We'll be right down, we tied a bunch of these vines together to form a rope," Olivia replied. Marcus then tied the vine rope around a large boulder and watched Olivia as she went down the vines first. Seeing she had made it into the room safely, Marcus then climbed down the vines after her.

When he got into the room, Olivia was staring wide-eyed at the Native writings on the walls.

"Wow, this is so cool!" she gasped. She then scanned the floor of the room and caught sight of the four skeletons. "Ew!" she shrieked, grabbing onto Marcus. "That is so not cool!"

"Damn," Marcus said, eyeing the skeletons. "This is wild; we're in like a tomb or something! Don't touch anything or we might be cursed!"

Olivia rolled her eyes and laughed. "Man, you watch way too many movies." She scanned the items more closely. "These items look pretty old, they might be worth something. What do y'all think?"

"Hell yeah," Marcus replied. "This could be some old Aztec stuff. We should sell it on eBay!"

"We're not going to be able to do anything until we get out of here, so let's go," Tim said. "Olivia, you go first."

"Ahem, why do y'all want me to go first? So you can look at my butt?" She smirked.

Marcus burst into laughter. "Girl, please! Just because you're Latina doesn't mean you got it going on like J.Lo!"

Tim laughed and playfully nudged Marcus. "For once, we're trying to be gentlemen, actually! You weigh the least, so can you please go?"

Olivia shrugged. "Whatever, perverts!" She began to climb up the vine but didn't realize the vine had come loose on the boulder. Halfway up her climb, the vine fell off the rock, causing Olivia to fall back into Tim's arms.

"See, what did I tell you? Perverts!"

Tim rolled his eyes and let her fall to the ground. "Do you still think I'm a pervert now?"

Olivia fell with a thud and coughed as dust rose up from the ground. "No, now I just think you're a jerk!"

They all peered up at the entrance to the underground room.

"Damn, we're screwed," said Marcus. "If we don't find a way out of here, we're going to end up like them," he added, pointing to the skeletons.

Tim frowned. "There has to be a way out of here. They had to get in here somehow. Maybe there's a secret passage or something."

All three of them began to examine the walls, hoping to find a way out. Tim chose the wall that looked like there were rocks up against it. Looking around for a lever for what seemed like hours, he finally threw his arms up in the air in frustration. "Man, we really are screwed!" He leaned on the wall and pressed his head against the rocks.

"Hey, wait. I can feel a little bit of a breeze here. I think there's something behind these rocks!" He called the other two over to where he was and confirmed the presence of a breeze. "I think that's how they got in here," he speculated. "Help me move these rocks. Let's see what is behind here… It might be our way out!"

The three of them began to dig and move the rocks around until they could see what appeared to be an opening into another tunnel. Tim climbed in to check if it was safe.

"This leads into another tunnel; let's keep digging!"

After an hour of digging, they finally made a hole big enough to fit all three of their bodies, and then each grabbed an artefact. Tim took the staff, Marcus grabbed the feathered crown, and Olivia draped the wolf's hide across her shoulders. As they made their way into the tunnel, Olivia started to hear a noise.

"Do y'all hear that?" she whispers. The others listened intently.

"It sounds like loud running water," Marcus said. "Hey, look! There's light up ahead!"

Overjoyed, the group broke into a jog. As they got closer,

the faint light ahead turned into a blurred clearing. The sound of rushing water was even louder.

Olivia pointed to the falls. "There's your running water right there, man! It's a damn waterfall and we're behind it!" They all walked right up to the entrance of the cave and looked at the falls.

"I'd say it was beautiful if I wasn't so damn tired and hungry," Olivia joked.

Tim suddenly felt a pang of hunger in his stomach. He hadn't noticed how hungry he was until Olivia had mentioned it. He looked around and noticed a stone path leading out of the falls.

"Let's follow that path. It looks like we won't get too wet if we go that way."

The others agreed and began to walk along the path.

"This path should lead us to dry land," Marcus said.

"I don't know about dry; it is raining, remember?" Olivia replied.

"Man, who cares! I just want out of this stupid cave," Marcus complained. Olivia nodded in agreement.

"Well, then let's stop complaining and do this, people!" Tim assured the group. He began to trek down the rocks with Olivia and Marcus in tow. Once they had come out from behind the falls, Olivia noticed it had stopped raining and that the sun was shining.

Marcus, however, could care less. "We're still lost!" he exclaimed.

"I think we should go west," Tim offered.

"How do you figure that?" Olivia asked skeptically.

Tim shrugged. "I don't know. It just feels right. I can't explain it."

"All right, then." Olivia sighed. She was too tired to argue. "We're right behind you, so lead the way."

They travelled west for about twenty minutes until Olivia suddenly came to a stop.

"What's wrong?" Tim asked.

"I thought I heard someone calling my name," she said. "Wait, listen!"

In the distance, faint voices could be heard: *"Olivia! Tim! Marcus!"*

Marcus grinned. "Hey, that's our classmates!"

"Make some noise so they can find us!" Tim said. The three started screaming and hollering to get the attention of their classmates. They could hear one student say, "Hey Mr. Goodwin, they're over here!"

They then heard Mr. Goodwin, their history teacher and organizer of the camping trip, yell out into the woods, "Hey everybody, we've found them!"

Within minutes, twenty five students were on their way

to Tim, Olivia, and Marcus's location. Before they arrived, Tim whispered to his friends, "Hey, let's keep all this crazy cave stuff to ourselves, all right?"

Marcus snorted. "You seriously thought I was going to tell people about a haunted cave with skeletons? Man, they would think I'm crazy! I sure as hell won't say jack."

"You can count me in too, my lips are sealed," Olivia promised.

"Good. It's just between us three, then," Tim said.

Right after their pact, Mr. Goodwin made his way over to the trio, looking very exasperated. "Are you children all right?"

"Of course, we're just a little hungry, tired, and embarrassed for getting lost," Tim said.

Their teacher lowered his voice to a hushed, serious tone. "Where the hell did you three take off to?"

Tim, unsure of what to say, stared at his teacher without an answer.

"We went to get firewood and got lost trying to get out of the storm." Olivia smiled.

A student from the crowd started to laugh. "Firewood, my ass." The group of students began to snicker.

Mr. Goodwin raised his eyebrow at the trio. "We'll keep this little firewood incident between us," he said with a grin. "We're leaving in the morning to go back home. Do you three think you can make it through the night without getting the urge to go collecting firewood again?"

Olivia was adamant. "Of course sir, we're done with firewood." Tim nodded his head.

"Now I know why black people don't camp out," Marcus said bluntly.

Mr. Goodwin shook his head and laughed. "All right, let's go campers!"

When they got back to the camp site, everyone was happy to see them. They were surprised to see they had become very popular while they were gone, but there were two campers who didn't join the celebrations—Josette Smith and Fatima Puja, both lovely young women. The two of them walked out in a huff. Marcus and Tim saw them leaving and quickly got up to go after them. Neither of them were dating, but there had always been a strong attraction between them. Josette was a dark-haired, blue-eyed beauty born and raised in the northwest. Her dad was into real estate and her mother was a homemaker. Together, they all lived in a Seattle suburb along with her younger brother, James. She was a very bright but insecure girl and had a hard time trusting boys because of a couple of bad relationships in her past. Even though she really liked Tim, she was afraid that she would get hurt in the relationship. Fatima, on the other hand, had long raven hair and green eyes. She was an olive-skinned beauty of East Indian descent, with a life very different from Josette's. She had only moved to Seattle six months prior from South Africa. Fatima's father was a surgeon and her mother was an interior designer. Her father had moved to the States to get away from all the corruption back in Africa and brought his family to the northwest for a fresh start. Her father was very strict and wanted her to focus more on school and less on social pleasures. Dating was an absolute "no" and a topic not up for discussion. Her mother was more of a free spirit and wanted her to enjoy the crucial social life so important to being a teenager—so long that it didn't interfere with her grades. She was the one working behind the scenes on trying to loosen up Fatima's father. Without her mother's help, Fatima would have never been allowed to go on the camping trip, which was her first. Many boys wanted to date Fatima, but with her father being so adamant about her not dating, it soon became a huge dilemma. Not even her mother could persuade her father otherwise. Indeed, Fatima was a good girl and did not want to upset her father, so she didn't bother with boys at all. Many of the boys thought she was a bit stuck up, but they didn't know what she would have to face at home. However, when it came to Marcus, she let her guard down just a little. There was something different about him. She found his "rough on the outside and caring on the inside" persona intriguing. She also loved his humor and honesty and found him pleasant to be around. The more she got to know him, the more she wanted to know. She truly enjoyed listening to his stories about his ghetto upbringing. It reminded her of the poor and suffering in Africa. She felt a connection with him and at times would let her guard down more than she had planned; however, she would always catch herself in the act and draw back. This always kept a distance between her and Marcus, causing him to wonder if he ever actually had a chance with her. The situation with Marcus lost in the woods and the fear of the unknown brought to light deep feelings in her heart and now she felt open and vulnerable. Seeing him return unharmed was very emotional to her—a part of her wanted to run and hold him, but yet another part was furious at the fact she could no longer control her feelings like before and that he had so stupidly put himself in the situation in the first place. Feeling the need to be alone to sort things out and get her emotions in check, she found a quiet, secluded area in the camp. Suddenly, Marcus ran up to her, out of breath.

"Hey, why did you run off like that?" he questioned. "Are you mad at me?"

Fatima glanced up at him and raised her eyebrow. "I wasn't in much of a celebratory mood," she replied icily.

"Okay," Marcus replied.

It was quiet for a moment.

"I can't believe you just ran off like that!" Fatima blurted. "Anything could have happened to you out there!"

Marcus laughed and replied with a sarcastic tone, "Hey you're right, I might have gotten eaten by a bear or a cougar out there." Noticing the unimpressed look on Fatima's face, he quickly added, "I'm just playing, girl!"

"I'm glad you think this is funny," Fatima said as she turned to walk away. Marcus grabbed her hand and pulled her back.

"Hey, please don't go. I'm sorry for making a joke of the situation. You're right," he began to say. "It was inconsiderate of me, but I have to be honest with you, I'm a little surprised to see how much you care about me. It's really kind of nice."

"Of course I care! Why wouldn't I?" Fatima replied.

Marcus shrugged. "You always give me mixed signals."

Fatima brushed her hair behind her ear. "Well, now you know, silly."

Marcus got very close to her—so close that their noses almost touched. "Well, I guess I do."

He put both hands around her waist. In the past, she would have pulled away, but right now she couldn't move. Her heart wouldn't let her. He stared at her intensely.

"Trust me baby, it's going to take more than just lions and tigers and bears to keep me away from you," he said.

"Oh my." She smiled. Marcus stared intensely into her eyes for a moment before cautiously drawing his face right up to hers and planting the softest of kisses on her lips. Because it was their first shared kiss, there was an almost euphoric feeling to it. The sweet open-mouthed kiss only lasted a few seconds, but it felt like an eternity. Marcus, being more experienced, was so caught up in the kiss that he almost slipped his tongue between her lips, but caught himself and slowly drew his lips from hers. He slowly opened his eyes and noticed that hers were still closed, as if she were savoring the moment.

"Wow," she breathed. "That was nice."

"I agree." Marcus grinned and leaned in for another kiss. Fatima extended a hand and placed it against his chest, stopping him in place.

"Hold on there, tiger," she said. "The rest you'll have to earn, and it's not going to be that easy."

"It's all good; I'm up for the challenge," Marcus replied.

"Good," Fatima said, then leaned in and kissed him on the cheek. "Then this one's a freebie."

Meanwhile, Tim had some sucking up of his own to do with Josette. Their situation was a bit different than that of Marcus and Fatima. Although Josette really liked Tim, she had some security issues and was scared that Tim would hurt her like others in her past had. It had been an uphill battle for Tim, who really liked her, but he was beginning to withdraw his feelings because he was losing hope. Yet here they were, with Josette beginning to walk away from the joyous camp reunion in a huff.

"Josette, please wait!" Tim yelled out, running after her.

"You insensitive jerk!" she hissed.

Tim, out of breath, stopped running. "Yes, you're right, I am an insensitive jerk. I'm so sorry, but we all got lost in that storm."

She turned toward him. "I'm sure your friend Olivia loved that."

Tim was silent until he realized what she was getting at. "Is that what this is all about?" he asked. "You know she and Marcus are my best friends—nothing more."

She turned her head away from him. "Well, maybe she didn't get the memo."

Tim laughed. "Well, here I was, thinking you were worried about my safety."

She shot a glance in his direction. "Shut up, you know I was." Suddenly, she quickly moved over to him and kissed him on the lips. "Do you believe me now?"

Tim stared at her in shock. A smile appeared on his face. "I need a little more convincing."

She kissed him again, but this time with more conviction. It felt heavenly, almost surreal. "The next time you want to go gallivanting in the woods and getting lost, it better be me getting lost with you."

Tim replied, "I promise," and they started to kiss again.

Over in another area of the camp, a few of the girls came up to Olivia and asked her if she was all right.

"Yeah, I'm all right. Thanks for asking," she told the group.

"So what's the deal?" one of the girls asked curiously.

Olivia raised her eyebrow. "What do you mean?"

"You know." They giggled and rolled their eyes. "Did you like, get with them?"

Olivia stuck her tongue out in disgust. "Hell no, what the hell are you girls smoking? I don't get down like that!"

"Well, how about a twosome?" another girl asked with a grin.

Olivia forcefully replied, "Look. Tim and Marcus are like brothers to me. You girls can keep your sick fantasies to yourselves, 'cause it isn't that kind of party!"

A few of the girls snickered. "Whatever you say, Olivia." They laughed sarcastically. As they walked off, Olivia rolled her eyes and threw her hands up in frustration.

After everyone had showered and finished dinner, the whole class joined each other around the campfire. Marcus faithfully sat beside Fatima while Tim sat next to Josette, with Olivia on his other side. Josette rolled her eyes at Olivia and gave her a bit of a sneer, wrapping her arm around Tim's and resting her head on his shoulder while staring directly at Olivia.

"Oh please, get a grip." Olivia sighed.

"Oh, trust me, I've got a grip—and it's a tight one," Josette replied. Both Tim and Olivia rolled their eyes. From across the fire, Marcus and Fatima—who had seen what happened—erupted with laughter. Fatima rested her head on his shoulder as he put his arm around her. At that moment, it was as if any walls between them had disappeared. They were closer than ever. It was now about 10 pm and it was dark, but the stars were out. The temperature had dropped, but the heat from the fire warmed the group. They had been talking about their plans for the future: graduation, prom, summer, and college for hours, until the conversation began to die down with the fire.

Noticing that people were starting to get sleepy, Tim spontaneously yelled out across the fire to Marcus.

"Hey Marcus, let's liven this party up! Can you give me a beat, man?" he yelled.

"Fo' sho, man!" Marcus replied, then broke into a beat box. Tim then started to sing the first few bars of the song "Stand by Me." Soon after, Olivia joined in with a few bars of the song. Before they realized it, the whole class was singing the chorus with them and clapping to the rhythm. Even Mr. Goodwin was singing along with the group.

After an hour or so, Tim was finally exhausted from the eventful day and decided to call it a night. Josette walked with him to his tent and gave him a kiss goodnight before he went in for the night. Tim held her tight before wishing her goodnight. Right behind them was Olivia and Marcus, who were also drained from their adventure. Marcus walked Fatima to her tent and gave her a big hug before saying good night and going back to his own tent. Behind them, Olivia giggled.

"Get a room!" she laughed.

Fatima laughed as well. "Not!"

Marcus shuffled his feet in embarrassment. "I wasn't even trying to go there anyway."

With a laugh, Olivia replied, "Sure you weren't, playa." Then she said to Fatima, "C'mon girl, let's go."

Fatima turned to Marcus and smiled. "Good night, then."

"Good night, baby," he said as he headed off to his tent. As the girls began to walk off, Olivia began to sing.

"It's just you and your hand tonight!" she sang at the top of her lungs. Both girls burst out laughing.

"Girl, you're so crazy!" Fatima laughed. Marcus, however, was not impressed.

"Why are you hating on me, sis?"

"Because you're corny," Olivia said. "Good night!"

"Yeah, whatever. Night," Marcus replied as he turned to walk away. He could still hear the two girls giggling as he went inside his tent.

Later that night, Tim was in the middle of an intense dream. He dreamt of Native warriors with anger in their faces; thousands of them marching to battle. In a flash, he heard loud screaming and a whirl of strong wind. The next thing he knew, the warriors were lying dead, spread out across the land as far as the eye could see. He turned around to see someone in the distance—it was a young boy who was crying, but Tim could not make out his face. He was holding something familiar. Tim traced back his memory to try to recognize the item. When he realized what it was, he was consumed with shock. It was the staff he had found back in the cave.

Tim woke up suddenly with his heart pounding and his body covered in sweat. The dream had seemed so real to him. He sat up and took a deep breath as he tried to gather himself together. He quickly looked over to the left of his sleeping bag where he had left the staff. He strained his eyes to focus in the dark light, but still could not see where he had left it. Suddenly, his heart stopped. It was gone. Jumping up, Tim started to check all over the tent for the staff. He grabbed his sleeping classmate and began to shake him to wake him up. "Hey man, have you seen the stick I had?"

Confused, his groggy classmate slurred, "Wh-what, man?" Oh... yeah man, we used it for firewood."

"What?!" Tim yelled angrily. "Why didn't anybody ask me first? You don't just take things that don't belong to you!"

The classmate, who was still half asleep, was not really paying attention to Tim. "Hey, chill out, man. Why are you losing it over a freaking stick, dude? Besides I did try to tell you, but you were passed out and mumbling crazy stuff. We needed the firewood—hell, wasn't that what you went looking for anyways?"

Frustrated, Tim stood up to leave the tent. "Whatever, just forget it." Leaving the tent, he headed over to the campfire to clear his head and sat down on a log where the raging fire had been burning earlier. Looking up at the stars, he glanced down to the fire pit. In the dim moonlight, he could see what looked like a stick lying in the pit. He moved closer to get a better look. Laying in the ashes of burnt wood was the staff—untouched and unscathed from the blazing flames. Tim couldn't believe his eyes.

How could this be? he thought to himself. He bent over to pick it up, shaking the remnants of burnt wood off the unscathed staff. "Well, at least it didn't burn up. Maybe it's more valuable than I thought."

He sat back down on the log with the staff resting on his lap. A cool breeze swept over the camp, causing Tim to shudder. As he sat there with the staff, Tim began to feel strange—it was almost euphoric. He closed his eyes as the cool breeze enveloped him, surrendering to sleep.

He dreamt of a long, long time ago, when the Natives ruled the land. He could see children playing in the fields while their mothers watched over them. He saw nature in all its beauty. Everything was peaceful. Suddenly, a faint voice in the distance was calling his name. It was getting louder...

"Tim!"

Tim opened his eyes to see Marcus standing over him. "Tim, man, wake up! Did you sleep out here all night?"

Tim rubbed his eyes and looked around. It was morning.

"No," he said slowly. "I came out here around three because I couldn't sleep. I guess I fell asleep out here."

"Yeah well, I didn't sleep well either," Marcus said. "I had this crazy dream that I could fly and man, did it seem real."

Olivia, who was also awake, came to the boys to say good morning.

"If you guys want to talk about weird dreams, I had a dream I was running with a pack of wolves!" She laughed. "Imagine that."

The trio was then interrupted by an announcement from Mr. Goodwin. "All right troops, pack all your things, it's time head home!"

Tim got up and stretched. "Well, it looks like it's about that time, guys. Let's get packing."

"I never thought I'd be saying this, but I'm kind of sad that we're leaving," Marcus said.

With a devilish grin, Olivia laughed. "Oh, really? I wonder why." Tim tried not to laugh, but couldn't help but chuckle.

"Yeah, I'm sprung. Tim, why are you laughing?" Marcus glared.

Tim held his hands out in surrender. "Hey, I didn't say anything!" he replied as he laughed harder.

"Whatever," Marcus said as he turned to go pack.

As the class began to load onto the bus, Tim stopped and turned to take in the scenery one last time. It was beautiful. On the bus, Marcus and Fatima were sitting together. She had rested her head on his shoulder, her hand holding his. She was content but had an air of sadness about her.

"Are you all right?" Marcus asked.

She shrugged. "Yes and no."

"Tell me why 'yes' and then why 'no.'"

"Well, the yes part is that I'm very happy we're closer," she began. "The no part is my dad. I don't want to upset him with this and I know he would flip out if he knew about us."

"Well, then he doesn't have to know right now," Marcus said. "We can keep this on the low so that we don't upset your folks. Look, we're both about to graduate and you're going away for school. Between now and then, I don't want any drama to come between us because I just found you and right now, I don't even want to entertain the thought of losing you. You feel me?"

Fatima smiled and squeezed his hand. "Yes, I feel you." She kissed him and he smiled.

"That's what's up," he replied smugly.

Tim had taken a seat next to Josette and they were holding hands. He was in a good place at the moment, but the events from the day before were still on his mind. Olivia was still thinking about the cave as well. As she was very superstitious, she believed that the cave was cursed. Her biggest concern was that they had disturbed some spirit by taking the three items. As she began to fidget with anxiety, she said a little prayer to calm her nerves.

Little did they know, the cave was only the beginning of a wild ride that would change their lives forever.

CHAPTER 3
Ebay and Beyond

The school trip was coming to an end. They were about ten minutes away from the school after the two hour bus ride. Tim was sleeping and resting his head on Josette's shoulder as she looked aimlessly out the window. Olivia was listening to music by herself while Marcus was holding hands and enjoying the moment with Fatima. Olivia saw that they were close to the school and realized that she should switch seats with Marcus so that when they reached the school, Fatima's parents wouldn't spot them together. She got up walked over to them.

"Marcus, I need to switch seats with you."

Marcus looked confused. "Why?"

"So Fatima's parents won't see you two sitting together and get any ideas."

"Oh yes! Sorry Marcus, she's right," Fatima said.

"Oh okay, I understand, but I just want to say before I go how much this–"

Olivia curtly cut him off. "Man, move your big head, you can mack later!" She grabbed his arm and pulled him out the seat.

"Damn girl, why you got to be grabbing all on me like that?" he joked.

"Fool, I'm trying to help you. If her folks see you and her sitting together, you'll be in deep crap, so you can thank me later."

He thought about the situation and agreed. "Yeah okay, I see. Good looking out." He backed up slowly, looking at her and then blowing Fatima a kiss. She reached her arm up as if to catch it, but at that moment, the bus hit a pothole and bounced hard, making Marcus fall and hit the floor. He stood up quickly and tried to be cool about it, but it was too late. The whole bus was cracking up.

"Wow, you really are falling hard for her, aren't you!" Olivia said as she and Fatima began to laugh.

"Whatever, hater," Marcus said, and then turned to Fatima. "I'll catch you later, baby."

"You haven't learned your lesson yet. You better sit your Don Juan butt down before you fall again, player!" Olivia laughed.

Marcus scowled at her before sitting down in his seat. The seat switch happened just in time because right as they pulled up on the school grounds, Fatima's folks were front and center waiting for them, as well as dozens of other parents. They all lined up to exit the bus, but Marcus made sure he was behind Fatima so they could secretly hold hands, low enough that no one could see. Fatima slipped her hand behind into Marcus's. He squeezed her hand gently. They both looked straight ahead with poker faces so as not to let on what was taking place at that moment. When they got off the bus, Tim gave Josette a quick hug before she had to head home. Marcus's grandmother was there to take him and Olivia home, while Tim's mom was waiting for him in the parking lot. When he got into the car, his mom smiled at his hug with Josette.

"Wow, she's a real cutie, son," she said.

With a huge grin, Tim peered out the window to get one last glance of her. "Yup, she sure is."

Later that night, Tim called Marcus and Olivia on a three-way call.

"What are you guys doing?"

"Working on a song," Marcus replied.

Olivia replied, "I'm just helping my mom cook dinner. What are you doing, Tim?"

"Just sitting here and thinking," said Tim.

"You're thinking about that cave, aren't you?"

"Well yeah, that and life in general," Tim said.

"Honestly, I can't get that cave off my mind either," Olivia admitted.

"Yeah, that cave scared the crap out of me, now that I think about it," Marcus chimed in.

"Do you think it was haunted by the spirits of the bodies that were in there?" Olivia asked nervously.

"I don't know, but something wasn't right," Tim replied.

"You can say that again, guys. If we never have to see that cave again it'll be too soon," Marcus said. Olivia and Tim agreed. Tim decided to switch the topic.

"Do you two want to meet over at my place after school on Monday to set up the eBay account and try to sell this stuff?"

"Hell yeah, time to get paid!" Marcus cheered.

Olivia was hesitant. "Sure, but what if this stuff is cursed? Have y'all thought about that?"

Marcus laughed. "Yeah and Rice Crispies really talk to me. Girl, you watch too many horror flicks!"

Frustrated, Olivia was adamant. "Well, we all know what we heard and saw in that cave, so you never know."

"Well, hopefully we won't have to hold on to the stuff for long enough to find out," Tim said. "Let's get real and get rid of it. We meet tomorrow my place, and don't forget to take pictures of the stuff so we can add them."

"Cool," Marcus said.

Olivia replied, "I'll be there and I hope you're right."

Tim had another dream that night, similar to the one he'd had after taking the staff, but this time there were Native men sitting in a circle around a fire. They were all chanting something in their native tongue, which he couldn't understand. Within the fire, there were forms and shapes made of flames. All of a sudden, a big storm with heavy winds ripped across the land, but the men still sat, chanting even louder as the weather engulfed them. Then, out of nowhere, a blast of wind knocked them all down and blew out the fire. All was dark.

Tim then woke up and sat up in his bed, his heart pounding and body drenched in sweat. The recurring dreams seemed so real and yet he didn't know what to make of them. In his heart, he knew there must be more to the dreams, but he couldn't connect the dots. Ten minutes later, he fell back asleep and slept peacefully through the night.

The following Monday, Marcus and Olivia met up with Tim at his locker before the school bell rang for their first class.

"Don't forget to meet at my house after school. We can meet up in the courtyard after and then head to my place," Tim reminded them. "Did you both bring the pictures?"

They nodded in agreement.

"Good, I'll see you both later," Tim said.

They all say goodbye and continued with their mornings, which for the most part, were very uneventful. Marcus and Tim had to give an oral book report for their English class, and Olivia, as usual, excelled in her baking class by making a three-tier wedding cake.

They met up again that day during lunch, but where the three of them would usually sit together now sat six. Fatima, Josette and Anthony—a boy who really liked Olivia, but she didn't see him in that way—were also at the table.

"Man, that camping trip was fun," Anthony started. "But you guys gave us a good scare! We thought Jason got you." As he chuckled, Marcus glanced over at Tim and shook his head. He turned back to Anthony.

"Man, you gotta stop staying up late watching old horror movies," he said.

After school, Marcus, Tim, and Olivia met up and headed over to Tim's house. Once there, Mrs. Wilson invited them to stay for dinner. They thanked her and accepted her offer, but went up to Tim's room first to set up the eBay account.

Olivia jumped on Tim's computer. "Okay, let's get this started. I'll need to upload all the pictures first."

They pulled up eBay and Olivia started to follow the directions laid out on the website on how to put an item up for auction.

"Damn," said Marcus. "Thank God you're setting this up, 'cause it is not as easy as I thought."

"Yeah, this is kind of confusing," Tim added. "What's a PayPal account?"

"It's almost like a merchant account," Olivia said.

"What's a merchant account?"

Frustrated, Olivia replied, "Man, you guys really need to read up on this stuff. I'll put it like this: it's where our money will be wired after someone buys our stuff."

"Okay, I got you, 'nough said." Marcus said.

"Now you two better be quiet and let me finish this!"

After 30 minutes, Olivia had everything set up and ready to sell.

"Let's leave it for a few days then check it and see who bites!" Tim said excitedly.

Both Marcus and Olivia agreed and they headed down to the basement to work on some music together. After an hour, Tim's mom called for them to come up for dinner. By this time, Tim's dad had come home from work and was already sitting at the head of the table, waiting to eat. Tim greeted his dad, saying, "Hi, dad."

"Hello, son," he replied.

Marcus and Olivia also greeted him. "Hi, Mr. Wilson."

"Hello, you two. You all sounded good downstairs." He smiled.

Tim's parents were very nice down-to-earth people, and

were very fond of Olivia and Marcus. While they were getting seated, Mrs. Wilson went to the kitchen to gather the food. Olivia tagged along to help her.

"Well, thank you, young lady," she said.

Olivia said, "No problem, Mrs. Wilson. I help my mom with dinner at home all the time."

"You're a great daughter."

Olivia smiled. "Thank you, I try."

They brought the food in and set it up on the table to the visible excitement of the men.

"Yum, fettuccine! It looks good, Mom." Tim drooled.

"I second that Mrs. Wilson, it looks and smells delicious," Marcus said.

Mr. Wilson added, "I'll have to agree with the boys, honey, it looks great. Thank you."

Modestly, Mrs. Wilson said, "Well, thank you all. I hope it tastes as good as you say it looks."

With a bit of a chuckle, they all dug into the meal. During dinner, Mr. Wilson asked Marcus and Olivia about their plans after graduation.

"Yes sir, I got accepted at Berkley school of music," Marcus said proudly. "I want to be a producer and recording engineer."

Mr. Wilson said, "Wow, that's great Marcus, congratulations! How about you Olivia?"

"I'll be studying to be a nurse; I got accepted at Johns Hopkins University." She smiled.

"That's great too," Mr. Wilson said. "Your folks must be so proud of you both. I'm proud of you all, and I'm happy to see my son's going to school for business."

Mrs. Wilson then said, "Speaking of school, have you both met Tim's new girlfriend?"

The others looked at each other, baffled. Mr. Wilson asked, "Who's this new girl, son?"

Olivia, with a devilish grin asked, "Yeah who is it? Marcus and I want to know, too!"

Looking a bit red in the face, Tim responded, "She's talking about Josette."

"I didn't know y'all were official," Marcus said.

"Me neither," Olivia agreed.

"Well, we're not. Not yet anyway. We're just starting to get to know each other better. Mom's just trying to make me blush," Tim said quickly.

Olivia laughed. "Well, I think it's working, cause you're turning menstrual red." She laughed out loud at her joke, but nobody at the table seemed to find it very funny. She quickly noticed and humbly added, "Sorry, just joking."

Marcus shook his head.

Tim quickly changed the subject. "What's for dessert, Mom?"

"Cheesecake," she replied.

"Yum, my favorite!" Olivia licked her lips. The boys nodded in agreement.

After dinner, Tim asked if he could borrow the car to take Marcus and Olivia home. Although apprehensive, his parents said yes, but reminded him to be safe. As a realtor, his father knew that area well, and although this wouldn't be the first time Tim had driven in that area, he still couldn't help but worry about him being there.

"Do you think we'll get lots of responses to our post?" Marcus asked on the way home.

"I don't know, but I think they should be worth something," Tim said.

Olivia was noticeably quiet. Marcus asked, "Olivia, why are you so quiet?"

"What, can't I be quiet?" Olivia snapped.

"Usually we can't shut you up!" Tim joked.

"Then don't complain, enjoy the silence," she said curtly.

Tim grinned and replied, "Okay, next topic."

What they didn't know was that Olivia—having a religious background—was still very disturbed by the events that transpired in the cave. She thought the cave was cursed, and that they might have been cursed as well.

Tim dropped Olivia off first since she lived only a few blocks away from Marcus, then dropped Marcus off and started home. As Tim was driving through their neighborhood, he looked around and saw drug dealers on the corner, garbage on the ground, and general despair around him. He couldn't help but feel fortunate for his circumstances, but at the same time he felt sad that his best friends had to live here in this environment. He felt a sense of hope knowing his friends knew they could do better and have the intelligence, vision, and strength to raise themselves up.

Fifteen minutes after getting home, Marcus called Olivia.

"Hey, what are you up to?"

"I'm just playing my guitar. Didn't I just leave you?" Olivia said.

"Well, I need a big favor," Marcus admitted.

"Sure, what's up?" she asked.

"Can you call Fatima for me on the down low?" he asked shyly.

In a slightly hesitant tone, she responded, "Yeah, I guess. Hold on, I'll three-way the three of us."

First she tried Fatima's cell phone, but got no answer, so she tried her land line. This time, Fatima's father picked up.

"Hello, who's calling?" he demanded.

"Good evening Mr. Puja, this is Olivia. May I please speak to Fatima?"

"Sure Olivia, just one moment."

He called for Fatima to pick up the phone. After a few minutes and sounding a bit out of breath, Fatima answered.

"I got it, Dad!" she shouted. Once he hung up, she asked who was calling.

"It's me, girl, Olivia. I have a special guest on the phone with me. Say hello special guest."

Then a voice Fatima knew oh-so-well came on and said, "Hello, beautiful."

Fatima, in a very happy tone, replied, "Well, hello there, handsome sir."

"This is already getting gross, so I'll let you two talk," Olivia said.

"If you hang up, we'll be disconnected!" Marcus said quickly.

Fatima then replied, "Marcus, give me 10 minutes and I'll call you back from my cell, because this line is not secure... If you know what I mean."

Marcus replied, "I sure do. Holler at me when you're ready."

"Okay, Olivia, I'll talk to you soon, sweets," Fatima said.

"You got it sis, peace out."

Around 20 minutes later, Marcus got his call.

"Sorry it took so long to get back to you, I had just gotten out of the shower when you both called."

Marcus replied, "Hey, it's all good, babe. I'm just glad you're here now."

"Me too, Marcus."

"We see each other in school and in passing, but I can't say I really know much about you other than that your dad's kind of mean," Marcus said.

She laughed at the notion. "No he's not, he's just very protective when it's comes to his little girl. He just wants the best for me and wants me to stay focused on my schooling. Now, in reference to what you were saying about you not really knowing much about me, what would you like to know?"

Marcus replied, "Anything and everything. Start from the beginning with your growing up in Africa."

Fatima took a deep breath. "Well, I had a good life as a child and had lots of friends, but all of a sudden, things started to go bad. There was a war and people were getting killed and the government was very corrupt. My dad didn't want any harm to come to his family, so we moved here to get away from all that and get a fresh start. My dad got a job at the hospital here and the rest is history."

"Wow, you've been through a lot."

"Well, I'll just say my life's been interesting to date. Now what about you, Mister? Who is the real Marcus?"

"Well, I was born and raised in the hood. I live with my mom, my two younger siblings, and my grandmother in a small apartment in a rough neighborhood."

"What about your dad?"

"I have a different father than my younger siblings and none of us know them. They've never wanted to be a part of our lives so all we've had was our family for support, mostly my grandmother and grandfather. After my grandfather died a few years ago, my grandmother moved in with us and she has been the biggest influence in my life. It's because of her that we all attend good schools."

"What does your mom do for work?"

"She's an LPN at the children's hospital."

"Hey, my dad works there too. Maybe they know each other."

"Hey, you never know, but it is a big hospital." He laughed.

"Yeah that's true," she agreed. "We've both had interesting lives, I see."

"Maybe that's why we were drawn to each other."

"Maybe, yes."

"Have you ever had a boyfriend?" Marcus asked nervously.

"Nope."

"All right, have you ever kissed a boy before?"

"Umm, yes, when I was like six years old!" she laughed. "But the first real kiss was with you."

"Oh wow, for real? I'm honored, but that didn't feel like a first kiss. It felt very natural," he said, shocked.

She replied, "Well, I do watch movies, you know." She laughed out loud and added, "I guess you can say I'm a quick study."

"Well, no more movie learning for you, from now on its only live action learning."

Laughing, she replies, "Okay, if you say so, Mister."

"Are you going to the prom?" Marcus asked suddenly.

"I really want to, but I'm not sure if my dad will let me go. My mom is working on him for me," she admitted.

"Damn, is he that strict?"

"Yes he is, unfortunately. But he's a good man; he just wants the best for me."

"Hey, I can understand that, but he's already raised a great daughter. I mean what more could he ask for? He should really lighten up," Marcus said cheerfully.

"I'm sure he will in time. He knows I'm not a little girl anymore."

"Man, I sure hope so. I'm going to have to ask for your hand in marriage one day and I don't want him to be tripping." Marcus laughed.

She blushed. "Oh really? Sounds like you have big plans there, Mister."

"Yup, and you're in them."

"Time will tell." She smiles. "So Mr. Sweet Talker, are *you* going to the prom?"

"Yes, that would be the plan."

"Are you taking anyone?"

He replied, "Well, since my girlfriend probably can't go with me, I'll probably go with a couple of my boys that are going solo."

"Who is this girlfriend you're talking about?" she asked.

"Look in the mirror and say cheese."

She laughed. "Okay!"

"Yeah I know, but if you do end up going, will you save me a dance?" Marcus asked.

She giggled. "I don't know, what would your girlfriend think about that?"

"She'd think I was having a great time." He laughed.

"Oh really?"

"Yup, my girlfriend is cool like that."

"Wow, she must be." Fatima chuckled a bit.

On the other side of town, Tim was calling Josette. She picked up the phone, sounding very happy to hear from him.

"What are you up to?" he asked.

"I'm just adding some new pictures of the camping trip to my Facebook page," she replied.

"Oh, cool," he said.

"Did you have a good time on the trip?"

"Yes, I did, especially near the end." He smiled and she agreed.

"So, Tim, are you going to the prom?" Josette asked shyly.

"I'm thinking about it. How about you?"

"I'm waiting for this one really special guy to ask me," she giggled.

Tim, a little bit confused, responded, "Oh, okay."

There was a pause on the phone for a second, followed by a chuckle. "Are you going to ask me or what?"

Relieved, Tim exhaled a bit. "Oh, I'm the really special guy?"

"Of course you are, silly, who else would it be?"

Tim laughed. "Okay then, will you go to the prom with me?"

"Yes, I thought you'd never ask." She giggled again.

"So does this mean you're ready to put your heart back on the market?" he asked.

She paused for a few seconds. "Yes, if you promise me you won't break it."

"Not a snowball's chance in hell would I hurt you."

"I believe you," she said sweetly. "So then, what's the deal with Olivia?"

"What do you mean by 'deal'?" Tim asked, confused.

"Well, I think she likes you," she said.

Tim laughed. "You're wrong. Olivia and Marcus are my closest friends and she's like a sister to me, so believe me there's nothing like that going on. You have to drop this and trust me,"

"Okay, okay. I do trust you," she said quickly.

"Thank you." He chuckled.

"I still don't like her," Josette mumbled under her breath. Tim sighed and rolled his eyes.

Meanwhile, miles away in another state, a man sat meditating in a dark, candle-lit room. The candles formed a circle around him in the middle of the room. He was in what seemed to be a deep trance. Without warning, the door to the dark room burst open and a man ran in.

"Sorry to interrupt you, Justin, but I have something very important to show you."

The man didn't respond at first. There was a bit of a silent standoff, and just as the man went to close the door, Justin came out of his trance.

"This better be really important," he said icily.

The man replied, "Oh, trust me, it is. I wouldn't have disturbed you otherwise."

"I'll be there in five minutes. It can wait until then, right?" he said as he stood up.

"Of course," the man said obediently as he closed the door behind him. Justin resumed his meditation, slipping back into a trance. Five minutes later, he came out of the room and entered an office where the other man was waiting for him.

"So where is this so important thing you wanted me to see?" asked Justin. The other man pulled up a page on eBay.

"Take a look at what's up for sale."

Justin looked on in disbelief, then rushed to get an old book he had kept locked up in a filing cabinet. He opened it and turned the pages until he came to page with a picture on it, then rushed to the computer to compare the eBay page with the book. He did this a few times, then realized the picture in the book and the item on eBay were one and the same.

"This can't be!" exclaimed Justin. "Finally, after all these years of searching and starting to believe it was only a myth, I see the legend is true."

"Whoever is selling these obviously doesn't know what they have or they wouldn't be selling something so precious this way," the other man said.

Justin agreed. The other man mentioned that the seller was in Washington State.

"Well I think we need to pay this person a visit. Book us two tickets to Seattle," Justin said without hesitation.

"Should I call the others?"

"No, not yet. We'll go first and try to retrieve it without conflict. Remember, this person probably doesn't know the power they hold, so we should take advantage of this fast. If it comes down to having to take it, then so be it," Justin said coolly.

The next day after school, Tim came home to see he had some traffic on the eBay account they set up. There was a message left for him by an archeologist and professor from a local college. He had left Tim his phone number and name, saying it was important he talk to him as soon as possible. Tim decided he would call him after dinner with Marcus and Olivia on the line to hear what he had to say.

Tim ran upstairs after dinner, curious and excited to hear what this man had to say. He called Marcus first; who in return called Olivia so they could all be on the four-way call. Tim told them about the email he received and that he wanted them on the phone to hear what the man had to say.

Tim dialed the professor. After two rings, a man picked up the phone.

"Hello, Tim. Thanks for the call."

Surprised, Tim asked, "How did you know my name?"

"It's called the magic of call display; that is, unless you're calling from someone else's phone," the man said.

"No, I'm Tim; and you are?"

"My name is Mitch Waters. I'm an archeologist and a professor at Goodwin University. My expertise is Native artifacts and relics. The reason I wanted to chat with you is to let you know that in order for you to get what's fair for your items, they first have to be authenticated so that you'll get a fair price from them and not be under bid for them," he said. "That is, if they're worth anything to begin with."

Tim and the others had not thought about this and asked the professor how they would go about getting them authenticated.

"We can test it here at the University. We have the equipment here to do so, and I have many other resources at my disposal," he said.

Skeptical, Marcus chimed in, "This sounds good and all, but what's in it for you? You aren't doing this for free."

"Well, I was hoping to make this somewhat of a partnership. I'll use my resources and expertise to help you get the most out of your find. Museums will pay a lot for a great find, and I have those types of contacts," Professor Waters replied.

"Do you have any stuff you found in museums now?" Olivia asked.

"I sure do. Feel free to Google me if you like," he said. What the professor didn't know was that Olivia was already searching him right at that moment.

"If he really is who he claims to be, then he's telling the truth about his stuff in the museums," Olivia said.

"Professor, how much of a cut did you want?" Tim asked.

"I think fifteen percent is a fair take, as well as a claim to the find along with you three," he said simply.

"What do you guys think?" Tim asked his friends.

"It sounds fair, but I don't know if we can trust you," Marcus said, still skeptical. Olivia agreed.

"I understand. To prove you can trust me, bring the items here and I'll test them anyway. You can decide what you want to do afterwards," Professor Waters said kindly.

"I think that's more than fair. What do you guys want to do?" Tim asked. Marcus and Olivia agreed to let the professor run some tests.

Marcus asked, "So Professor, do you think they're worth a lot?"

"It's hard to say without examining them. Why don't you all come by the school tomorrow with the items and let me get a look at them? Does six-thirty work?" he replied.

"It works for me," Tim said.

"I have a basketball meeting, but we should be done in time for me to make it," Marcus said.

Finally, Olivia agreed as well, "Yeah, I'm in."

"Then we're all agreed?" asked Tim.

"Yeah," Marcus and Olivia said together.

"All right then. Olivia, you and I can hang out at school until Marcus is done with his meeting, then we can all take it from there."

"Excellent," said Professor Waters. "I'll see you tomorrow, then."

The three students all agreed and said their goodbyes to the professor before hanging up.

Almost an hour later, Tim got a mysterious phone call with a long distance number on the call display.

Tim answered the phone. "Hello?"

"Are you the person selling the items on eBay?" the voice said icily.

Tim replied, "Yes that would be me."

"I'd like to make you an offer for them. How does five thousand sound?" the voice asked.

Caught off guard, Tim stood in shock. "Oh wow, it sounds really good, but I can't say yes right now because I'm in the middle of getting them authenticated. I should have an answer for you in a few days," he said.

The voice on the other end very persistently replied, "I'll give you ten thousand for just the staff, by itself, as is."

Enthused, Tim exclaimed, "Wow! I'm really flattered, and it kills me to say this, but I have to wait a few days before I can answer."

There was a moment of silence and then the voice on the other end responded in a dark manner, "You silly boy. I gave you a chance to give me what should rightfully be mine. Now, I shall have to take it from you." The line went blank. He had hung up.

Tim was a bit shaken by the tone and threatening manner from which he ended the conversation, so he put on his headphones and cranked up his music to try to take his mind off the call until he fell asleep.

The next morning before heading to school, Tim let his parents know he was going to hang around after school to watch the soccer team play, so he would be late for dinner. Once he got to school, Marcus and Olivia met up with him at his locker.

"I got good news and not so good news," he said slowly.

"What do you mean?" asked Olivia.

"Well, the good news is this stuff is definitely worth a lot of money, because I got a call last night from someone offering me ten thousand dollars for the staff alone."

Excited, Marcus interrupted him. "WHAT! Are you serious?" He and Olivia both started jumping up and down in excitement.

"What did you say?" Olivia asked enthusiastically.

Tim responded, "I told him I'd have to get back to him on it."

Marcus paused for a second. "Man, are you crazy? Why didn't you take the money?"

"Yeah man, what are you smoking?" Olivia agreed.

Tim replied, "You two need to stop and think about this for a minute. This guy seemed really anxious to take the stuff as is, which leads me to believe he was trying to low ball me on the price. Now, I'm sure they're all worth way more than he was offering."

"Yeah, that makes sense," Olivia thought out loud.

"Okay, now that we know they're worth something, what was the bad news?" Marcus asked.

"The dude lost it on me and then threatened to take them anyway, and he sounded like he meant it." Tim gulped.

"Well he's got to take them from all three of us and that isn't going to be easy," Marcus said adamantly.

"You're damn right," Olivia added. Right then, the school bell rang and they had to head off to their first class.

"We'll pick up on this later," Tim said quickly. The others agreed and made their way to class.

After school, Tim, Marcus, and Olivia met up and headed over to the University to see Professor Waters with the items they found. Their first impression when meeting him was that he seemed nice and very professional. After greeting them, he asked if he could see the items, so they pulled them out and set them on the table.

The professor picked them up one by one and examined them. Even from a first glance, he could tell there was some history to them. He started to do a few basic tests on them and took samples to do more in-depth testing. They would have to be sent out for analysis.

"I definitely think you have something here," he said, amazed. "Where did you find these items?"

"We found them in a cave when we were on a school camping trip," Tim replied.

"It would really help me if I could see that cave. Do you think you can you take me back to it?" the professor asked.

Worried, the three of them exchanged glances. "I guess we can," Tim said hesitantly.

"Thank you. That will really help me to determine more about where these relics originated."

After an hour, the three kids had to get home, so the professor took some pictures and had them all agree to a date and a time to visit the cave.

"I'll come pick you all up around seven in the morning this coming Saturday," he told them. Tim, Marcus and Olivia reluctantly agreed and then drove home with the relics.

On the drive home, Marcus spoke up, saying "Man, I can't believe we agreed to go back to that haunted cave!" He gulped.

"Yeah, I know," Olivia said slowly. "I still think it's cursed."

"Well, if we want to get the most out of this, we need to do it. Plus, you never know, maybe it was a one-time occurrence," Tim said hopefully.

Marcus and Olivia both looked at each other and shook

their heads.

"Plus, deep down inside, aren't you curious to find out more about what happened and why?" Tim asked them.

"No!" Marcus and Olivia said at the same time.

Under his breath, Tim said to himself, "Well, I am."

CHAPTER 4
Chance Meeting

Before the kids could keep up with the week, Saturday had arrived. As promised, Professor Waters was there first thing in the morning to pick up the kids. On the drive there, everyone was quiet, and he was first to break the ice.

"So you all are graduating this year? You must be excited," he said.

"Yeah," Marcus said unenthusiastically.

The professor thought their reactions were odd, but figured it was because it was early in the morning and they were all just tired.

"Don't you have prom coming up?" he asked.

"Yup," Marcus said bluntly.

"I'm going with my lady," Tim said proudly.

Olivia sighed. "Oh God, here we go."

"Lucky you. At least you can pick her up at her front door. I have to cross my fingers that mine can even go and if she does, I'll have to meet up with her at the prom," Marcus retorted.

Tim thought for a moment. "Yeah, that does suck," he said.

"Fatima and I talked last night and she *is* going," Olivia said.

All of a sudden, Marcus's face lit up. "WHAT! She's going?" he asked excitedly.

"Yup," Olivia said, amused.

An excited Marcus responded, "That's hella cool!"

"She's supposed to call you when we get back home to tell you the news, so when she does, act surprised," Olivia said.

Marcus replied, "I can do that. Thanks for the heads up, sis."

"No problem, that's what best friends are for." She smiled.

Finding their talk amusing and reflective, Professor Waters smiled. "It's so exciting to be young!" he said. "By the way, I'm excited to see this cave you found this stuff in. You three may have stumbled on more than you know."

"That's what we're afraid of," Olivia mumbled.

"What was that, Olivia?"

"Oh nothing, just talking to myself."

"Um, okay," Professor Waters responded.

They all became quiet again. They began to think that the professor may have been stumbling into what they found on that first encounter and they would rather not be going back. But deep down inside, a part of them craved answers too, despite being scared. Professor Waters was starting to sense their anxiety, so he tried to break the silence and tension in the car.

"Hey, do any of you know any fun long distance driving songs?" he asked.

They all looked around at each other, but before they could say a word, Professor Waters broke out into song:

"One hundred bottles of beer on the wall, one hundred bottles of beer, if one of those beers should happen to fall, how many bottles of beer on the wall?"

Olivia rolled her eyes as he continued to sing.

"Ninety-nine bottles of beer on the wall, Ninety-nine bottles of beer, if one of those beers should happen to fall, how many bottles of beer on the wall?"

Instead of joining in, Marcus abruptly cut him off. "No disrespect, Professor, but we aren't with it," he laughed.

Professor Waters replied, "Oh, I'm sorry; I just thought I'd try to loosen things up; you all seem a bit tense. Is everything all right?"

"Yes, we're all just thinking about grad and everything," Tim lied.

"Oh okay, I guess I can understand, I've been there, too," Professor Waters replied.

Marcus, sitting on the passenger side, asked the professor if he could throw in a CD.

"Sure," said Professor Waters. Marcus took one out of his bag and put it in. The groove from the song had them all bopping their heads and tapping their feet.

"Who is this?" Professor Waters asked.

"It's us!" Olivia laughed.

Professor Waters, being totally surprised, responded, "Wow, are you serious?"

"Yes sir, I'm in the middle of mixing it and just wanted to see if y'all liked it so far," Marcus said proudly.

"That's really great. You guys are very talented!" Professor Waters exclaimed.

"Thanks," the kids all said at once.

"Do you guys mind if I put on some music as well?"

"Hey it's your car," Marcus said.

Professor Waters went ahead and turned on the radio to his favorite station. Country music filled the car.

Under his breath Tim looked at Olivia and said, "Man, this is going to be a long ride."

"Who you telling?" Olivia replied.

A couple of hours later, they arrived at the campgrounds and ended up parking close to where the class was when they were there. They grabbed the relics and all their gear and started the hike toward the cave. While the professor was curious and excited to see the cave, the other three were quiet and hesitant. They didn't want to be going back to this cave, and they were trying their best not to let it show, but the closer they got, the more it was obvious that they were very uncomfortable. By then, the professor knew something was up and wanted to ask if there was something wrong, but didn't want to agitate them anymore.

Olivia was the first to break the silence. "It's over there," she said quietly, pointing in the direction of the cave.

Professor Waters looked up to see waterfalls ahead. He looked around for a cave, but didn't see one.

"Where?" he asked.

"The cave is behind the falls," Tim answered.

"Oh, okay. Lead the way, my young friends," Professor Waters said enthusiastically.

The three paused for a second, looked at each other, took deep breaths, and began to walk on. They started to climb the rocks leading up and behind the falls, then entered the caves. Once inside, they pulled out their flashlights, but then noticed that the torches they left were still lying on the ground at the cave entrance.

"Hey, maybe we can use these again and save our batteries," Tim suggested. The others agreed.

Professor Waters briefly examined the torches. "Did you find these torches in the cave?" he asked.

Tim replied, "Yes, why?"

"Torches like these date back to the eighteen hundreds," he said. "I think you really found something here."

"How can you tell?" asked Tim.

"Because, young man, this is what I do for a living. I've found these types of artefacts on digs quite often."

The excitement in his voice was evident, but the others didn't share the enthusiasm. They wanted to get in and out of there as soon as possible. The deeper they dwelled in the cave, the tenser they became. Professor Waters noticed this and decided to ask what was wrong.

Olivia hunched her shoulders. "Umm, I don't know."

He looked over at Marcus and Tim and they made the same gesture. With that response, the professor decided to leave it alone and just move on. As they kept walking, the three noticed things seemed good so far; there were no ghost sounds or cave shaking. They approached the entrance of the room where they found the relics and start clearing some rocks that that had fallen and were blocking the way into the room. Once they got enough clearance, Professor Waters went in first, the others in tow. He was amazed by the old drawings on the wall and immediately started to take pictures of the walls and the rest of the room, then examined the skeletons dressed in old Native clothes. He took notice that one was wearing the headpiece and emblems of a chief. He proceeded to take pictures of the skeletons and examined their handmade water containers, food pouches, and weapons. He took note of the altar the relics were found on, then turned to the wall and attempted to translate what the drawings meant. All he could decipher was that there was a war between tribes over the great power of the staff. Many died in that war and it was because of its power that the staff had to be hidden. Professor Waters then asked to see the staff. He noticed an inscription in an old Native text. As he looked closer at it, he saw that it said, *"Only the pure of heart can be worthy."*

Professor Waters had a hard time believing what he was reading. It was a tall tale that the Native people had passed on for generations.

"I think you guys really stumbled on something special here. There are even more artefacts here than the items you found. We'll share in those too and if things pan out like I think, your college educations should be paid for and then some!" Professor Waters said ecstatically. "I need to get these back to the school to research them, but in the meantime, let's keep this between us. You should probably take your ad offline. If I don't get back to you by next week, then sell them to whoever you wish."

Marcus, Tim, and Olivia all agreed.

"Okay, let's pack up some of this stuff and get out of here," Professor Waters said.

All of a sudden, they started to hear the faint chanting again.

"Did anyone else hear that?" Professor Waters turned around and the kids were already running out of the room and back into the cave. The professor thought that was odd, but before he could think further, the cave started to shake and rumble. In an instant, he realized why they were acting the way they were and started running himself. They didn't stop running until they were once again at the entrance to the cave.

As they all stood there panting and out of breath, Professor Waters asked, "What the hell was that?"

"W-we don't know," Olivia stuttered.

"Is that the reason you all seemed so tense on the way here?" the professor asked.

All together, they nodded their heads.

"We didn't say anything because we didn't want you to think we were crazy," Olivia said. "I personally think it's cursed and that it has something to do with this stuff we found."

"Well, I don't know what that was, but I know it wasn't normal. I've been doing digs for years and I've never come across this type of activity. I'll try to get some answers when I look more into this. Let's grab this stuff and head back."

They all started their climb down the rocks and then on to level ground, back to the campground where they began. Around fifteen minutes into their walk back, they came across two mysterious men. Both men looked to be of Native decent. One was extremely tall at nearly 6'6 and had dark eyes with black, slicked-back hair. He was dressed casually in all black, with his long black trench coat standing out with the odd-looking necklaces he wore. The other man was shorter and had short dark hair, an olive skin tone, and very bad acne. He was dressed a little more averagely, with blue jeans, a jean jacket, and dark T-shirt. He had a sinister look on his face. They both looked out of place and that made the face-off feel weird. Standing a cautious fifteen feet away or so from the men, Professor Waters engaged them by saying hello.

The taller man spoke first, "Good afternoon, gentlemen and lady. Lovely afternoon, wouldn't you say?"

The shorter man beside him displayed a devious grin, then the taller one motioned at the relics. "Now, what do you have there?"

Tim recognized his voice. "Hey, you're that creepy guy who called me the other night and wouldn't take no for an answer!"

"Do you remember what I said before I hung up?" he hissed.

All of a sudden Professor Waters recognized the tall one. "Oh my God. It's Justin Sigo."

"Professor, you know this man?" Marcus asked, confused.

"I know of him. He's one of the biggest collectors of Native artefacts in North America, and he's very wealthy," Professor Waters said.

"You would be correct. It's me in the flesh. I tried to share the wealth with your young friends for the staff, but he would not sell it to me," Justin said.

"What are you doing out here?" Professor Waters asked him.

"I've come to retrieve what's mine."

"Like hell you are," Marcus spat.

"Justin, are you serious?" Professor Waters asked, confused.

"I'm dead serious. You won't get out of these woods alive unless you hand over the relics—starting with the staff—right now," he said angrily.

"What are you going to do if we don't?" Marcus argued. "Cause how I see it; it's all of us against you and your boy."

Justin let out a loud laugh as he and his sidekick pulled out two enormous knives.

"No, I think the odds are in our favor, homeboy."

"OH DAMN!" Marcus yelled.

"Run, kids!" Professor Waters yelled. They all started to run, but Justin and his sidekick did not chase after them immediately.

"Let them run. They won't get too far," He hissed.

Meanwhile, Professor Waters and the others were running through the woods, scared for their lives.

"If they catch up to us, we should split up and meet back

at the car, I have a two-way radio and one of us can call the police!" Professor Waters yelled out.

They stopped to take a quick breath, panting and scared.

"I don't hear them, I think we lost them," Tim said quietly.

Out of nowhere, a hissing voice came from behind them. *"Oh, but we found you."*

They spun around and about ten feet away were Justin and his associate.

"Oh shit!" Marcus screamed. Justin laughed and began to walk toward them.

"We're out!" Marcus yelped, and they all started running again.

"Split up!" the professor yelled.

Marcus and the professor ran to the left while Olivia turned right. Tim ran straight with Justin in tow. Justin's associate went after Marcus and Professor Waters. Olivia jumped into a bush and hid while Justin ran past her in his pursuit of Tim. She saw a big stick by the bush, not far from where she was hiding, and grabbed it quickly as she started to run in the same direction as Justin and Tim. She hoped to sneak up on Justin so she could club him over the head.

Meanwhile, Justin's associate was being outrun by Marcus and Professor Waters.

"Hey, he can't even keep up with up us!" Marcus yelled.

"It doesn't matter, just keep running!" the professor yelled back.

Marcus then stopped to look back and yell, "Fool, you should have eaten your Wheaties!"

A deep growl resonated from behind them.

"How about I just eat you both?" The man growled at them.

Marcus looked back again only to find the man transforming into a cougar. Despite their efforts, they couldn't outrun the gigantic cat. Now, almost out of breath and sore all the tree branches beating at them as they ran into wove between and around the trees, they began to slow down. Marcus again took a quick look over his shoulder, and in that instant, the cougar jumped into the air, headed right for him. In the excitement, Marcus lost his footing just as the cougar was about to land on him, but before he could hit the ground, the crown of feathers he wore on his head began to expand and sprout more feathers, covering his body from his head down. His outstretched arms began to move up and down as if flapping, and a beak started to extend from his face. Marcus had changed into a giant eagle. He soared into the air, leaving the cougar to miss him and land on Professor Waters. The professor didn't see the transformations of either one of them because his back had been turned.

Professor Waters was lying on his back, trying to fight off the cougar that was hovering over him and frantically trying to claw and bite him. Though it lasted only seconds, it seemed like an eternity. All of a sudden, a big shadow loomed over them both and in an instant; something lifted the cougar off of the professor and flung it into a nearby tree. Amidst of all the excitement, it took him a few seconds to realize that it had been a huge eagle that had grabbed the cougar and now it seemed to be coming at him too. He scrambled to get up and started running, but didn't get far before the giant eagle swooped down and grabbed him, flying high into the sky.

Shaken up and back in his human form, all their pursuer could do was watch angrily as they escaped. Confused and scared, Professor Waters tried to wrap his head around what was happening. At the same time, he was worried sick about Marcus. He did not know was that the eagle was, in fact, Marcus.

Meanwhile, Justin was in hot pursuit of Tim. Olivia was swiftly following them with the large stick she had found.

"Why is this stick so important to you?" Tim yelled frantically.

"Boy, if you only knew! But I tire of these games. You should've taken the money when you had the chance!" Justin yelled angrily.

Justin began to mumble something in a Native tongue while clutching what looked like to be an old necklace. All of a sudden, he dropped down to the ground and began running on all fours. His face began to change rapidly: Justin's eyes and ears grew much larger; his bared teeth sharpened and elongated to become fangs. His hands became enormous black paws, covered in hair that began to sprout from the rest of his quickly expanding body. As he grew larger, Justin's clothes began to tear and fall from his form until he finished morphing into a huge grizzly bear. Olivia, who was watching the scene from behind, looked on in disbelief at the bear.

"What the hell!" she exclaimed. She dropped to her knees and began to pray.

Tim heard a growling sound behind him and glanced over his shoulder to find a grizzly in pursuit of him.

"Oh shit, where did that come from?" he yelled, not knowing that the grizzly was Justin. Tim panicked and started to run faster. Not paying attention, he tripped over a tree root and fell to the ground, rolling several times before ending up on his back. Looking up, he saw the bear charging at him. Quickly, Tim covered his face with one arm and held the staff up with the other in an attempt to protect himself. In that moment, his heart was racing and pounding as he prayed aloud. Unbeknownst to him, the staff had created a barrier of wind between himself and the bear. The bear was growling, clawing and snapping at Tim, desperately trying to get him, but couldn't penetrate the barrier.

Meanwhile, Olivia approached the bear. From behind, she couldn't see the barrier between the bear and Tim. Thinking the worst, she charged forward with the stick in hand, going a few feet before falling on all fours. The wolf's hide she had wrapped around her shoulders grew until it covered her entire form and transformed her into a huge white wolf.

After a few minutes of feeling the bear's presence and hearing it growl around him, Tim started to wonder why it wasn't striking him and cautiously moved his arm back a little to take a peek. In that split second, a huge figure had knocked the bear over. Tim grabbed the opportunity and got back up on his feet only to find a big white wolf standing between him and the bear. Confused and scared, he contemplated running but realized there was no way he could outrun either animal. He held the staff up like a baseball bat and took a defensive stance, not knowing that the white wolf was Olivia. They all stood there, not moving for what seemed like hours. Finally, as the bear was readying to charge at them both, Tim realized that the wolf was trying to protect him. The wolf would growl at the bear but then turn to Tim in a non-aggressive manner that had a sort of calming effect on him. The bear began to circle the two, looking to attack, mimicking the movements that Tim and the wolf made. The wolf then bumped Tim with its rear, then turned and looked at him as if it was trying to tell Tim something. It bumped him a second time and looked at him while motioning its head. Tim began to think the wolf was motioning him to get on its back. Reluctantly, Tim slowly began to climb on top of the wolf. Right at that moment, the bear began to charge at them, but now with Tim securely on its back, the wolf took off like a rocket through the woods. It was so fast, all the bear could do was watch them go.

Meanwhile, the professor finally opened his eyes. In the distance, he could see his truck as the eagle began to descend. Now, he realized the eagle was not going to kill him, but was taking him to his truck. The eagle had saved him. Now, Professor Waters couldn't help but feel a sense of dread at not knowing what happened to Marcus and the others. He would never forgive himself if anything had happened to any of the kids because he was the one that brought them there. How would he tell their parents that he was responsible for their deaths? All these things on his mind left him with a heavy heart, so he began to pray. Soon, the eagle, with the professor in tow, approached the truck. Once low enough to the ground, the eagle dropped him a few feet away. The momentum of him hitting the ground caused him to tumble a few times. Once he stopped rolling, a banged-up professor watched the eagle attempting to land a few feet ahead, but something strange happened in the midst of its landing. It began to take on a human form right before hitting the ground. Professor Waters was stunned by this occurrence, but even more stunned when he realized that it was Marcus who had transformed into the eagle. A groggy and confused Marcus sat up to find the professor sitting up on the ground, staring at him with a gaping mouth.

"How did we get back here?" he asked.

"Trust me, you don't want to know," the professor answered, still wide-eyed.

All of a sudden, Tim burst through the trees on a large wolf. Marcus and the professor turned to each other and shared a glance before looking back at Tim and the oncoming wolf. Just as they thought it was too late, the wolf began to morph underneath Tim, making him tumble forward onto his face. He turned around quickly, barely catching the final transformation of the wolf morphing back into Olivia. Once back to normal, a confused-looking Olivia glanced at Tim, only to receive the same expression back. They both looked over to Professor Waters and Marcus on the ground, staring at them with that same bewilderment.

After a few moments of silence, Olivia yelled out, "What the hell!"

"How did you do turn into that wolf?" Tim asked, shocked.

"Hell, I don't know, man!" she stuttered back.

"This is crazy!" Marcus said.

"How could this be?" Tim asked.

Professor Waters stopped to gather his thoughts, then looked over at the feather crown on Marcus's head and the white wolf's hide draped around Olivia.

"It's these artefacts you found! They must have some kind of power, and that's why Justin wanted them so badly," he said, bewildered.

"Well, he seemed to really want the staff, which means it must be extra special," Tim said.

"How will we find out?" Marcus asked.

"I know just the person who can tell us," replied the professor. "Chief Ahote of the Mowakin tribe can help us. He is old and wise and knows his people's history inside out. But let's get out of here before they come back to finish the job," he quickly added.

"Yeah true that; let's bounce," Marcus agreed.

They all headed over to the park ranger station and informed the ranger of the two men that had chased them through the woods with knives. They identified one of the men as Justin Sigo. The ranger called the police and as a group, they all went back to where they had run into Justin and his henchman. However, they were gone and not a trace of them remained.

The police then tracked Justin down, only to find out he had an alibi. He had at least six people who agreed that he was in a meeting all day and couldn't have driven out there and back in between meetings. The police could do nothing but take down the kids' and professor's phone numbers and names in case they found someone in the park who fit the description of the men who had chased them.

Tired and weary, all the group could do was head back home. On the drive home, everyone was quiet and seemed to be in deep thought about the day's events. Professor Waters was the first to break the silence.

"Let's keep this between us until I can come up with some answers, all right kids?" he said. "I'll develop the pictures I took and talk to Chief Ahote. I'll get back to you by the week's end. In the meantime, be careful and keep those relics out of sight. If you see Justin or any of his friends, call the police immediately."

The others nodded their heads in agreement as they continued the drive. The rest of the trip was pretty quiet and somber to say the least; no one said a word except for goodbye as they were dropped off at home one by one.

Later that night, Tim had another vivid dream. He was walking through a meadow with dead bodies sprawled all across the ground in front of him. The trees were uprooted and broken. He heard crying and turned to see where it was coming from. On the hill, he noticed a boy in his mid-teens on his knees crying, holding the staff in one hand and using the other hand to wipe his tears. His head was faced down, but as Tim got closer, the boy raised his head to look right at him.

Tim woke up to find himself crying. He could feel the boy's intense pain rippling through his body, but he still couldn't make a connection with him. He wondered why he was having these dreams and what the meaning behind them all was. What did the staff have to do with his dreams? Who was the boy? There were too many questions and no answers. He gathered his thoughts and fell back to sleep.

On the other side of town, Olivia was praying by the side of her bed for God to protect her and her friends. Marcus was home playing video games until his mother yelled at him to go to bed. He couldn't sleep and the games helped to take his mind off what happened earlier in the day. Eventually, they all fell asleep.

Miles away in a candlelit room, Justin Sigo sat in a deep trance. As he came out of the trance, his eyes were black and angry. He would not rest until the staff of power was his.

His sharp voice echoed throughout the room: "Soon we will be one, and I'll bring the world down to its knees." He let out a devilish laugh into the night.

CHAPTER 5
The Calm Before the Storm

The next day, Tim dragged himself out of bed and to get ready for school. He didn't sleep well, so he hoped a good shower would wake him up. After a hot shower, he got dressed and went off to school.

At school, Olivia and Marcus met up with Tim at his locker. "What's up?" Marcus asked.

"Not much," Tim replied. "Did you two sleep well?"

"Not really," said Marcus.

"Nope, did you?" Olivia added.

Tim shook his head. "Not really." Just then, the bell rang, and Tim turned to leave. "I'll talk to you guys later." Marcus and Olivia said their goodbyes as well and headed off to class.

Later, they all met up at the school cafeteria for lunch. After they sat down together, it was quiet for the first few minutes, but then Marcus spoke up. "Look, we can't sit here and pretend that the other day didn't happen. We need to talk about this."

Before he could say more, Josette came up behind Tim,

wrapped her arms around his neck, and kissed him on the cheek. "Hello, handsome!" she said.

"Hey, beautiful," Tim replied. At the same time, Fatima came over to sit with Marcus.

"Hey, girl," she said to Olivia, then looked to Marcus and asked, "Did you miss me?"

"No doubt," he replied. "Did you miss me?"

"Maybe," she replied with a smile on her face. "So how was your weekend?"

"Interesting," Marcus replied.

"How so?"

"Yeah, tell me about your weekend trip!" Josette jumped in.

"It wasn't too exciting," Tim said. "We just came across a bear and got chased."

Both Fatima and Josette gasped and said, "Oh my God! Are y'all okay?"

"Yeah," Marcus said. "We flew the coop, so to speak." He and Tim both let out a chuckle.

"Yup, we outran him," Tim added.

Then Marcus added, "Olivia ran like Flo Jo."

Both boys laughed again, but Olivia didn't. In an angry tone, she replied, "Well, if I ran like Flo Jo, I guess we can say you flew like an eagle, right?"

Marcus immediately stopped laughing. "Okay, okay, I get your point."

"Good!" Olivia said. "Now both of you can cut it out!"

Fatima and Josette joined in, Fatima saying, "This is not funny. One of you could have gotten hurt!" And Josette chiming in, "That's right, this is nothing to joke about."

"You're right," said Tim, "And we're sorry. Right, Marcus?"

"Yeah, my bad," Marcus said. They continued to eat their lunch in silence.

By the time Friday rolled around, nobody had heard from the professor. Olivia and Marcus met with Tim in front of his locker at school, and Marcus asked, "Have either of you heard anything from the professor?"

"No, have you?" Tim and Olivia asked.

Marcus shook his head. "No, that was why I was asking y'all."

"I sure hope he's okay," Olivia said.

"I'm sure he's fine," Tim said. "He'll call when he has something to tell us."

"Yeah, I'm sure you're right," Olivia said. Then, just as they were about to head off to class, Josette ran up to Tim and asked what he was up to during the weekend and if he was free to come to dinner at her place.

"Sure," Tim said, "What time do you want me to be there?"

"Dinner is at six, and we can see a movie after."

"Cool! So what do you wanna see?"

"It doesn't matter," Josette said, smiling brightly. "Not as long as I'm with you. So you pick."

"You're sweet. I'll find something good," Tim said.

"Okay, I'll see you tomorrow then!" Josette said happily.

"Okay. Should I bring something?"

"Nope, just bring your fine self."

Tim chuckled. "Okay, I'll be there. Hope your folks like me."

"Oh, they will," Josette said, and winked.

At lunch, everyone met up again. Josette explained to the group how excited she was about going on her first official date with her new boyfriend, to which Olivia rolled her eyes.

"Wow, that must be nice," Marcus said. "I sure wish I could take my girl to the movies."

Not knowing Fatima's family situation, Josette asked, "Why don't you two double date with us?"

All of a sudden everybody got quiet and looked away. When Josette saw this, she asked, "Why does everyone have that look on their faces?"

"Well, my family isn't too high on me dating," Fatima said.

"Oh!" Josette said. "Well, maybe they don't have to know!"

"Well, I really don't like lying to them..."

Josette clicked her tongue and rolled her eyes. "Well, how can your relationship grow if you can't spend quality time together?" she asked.

Fatima stumbled on her words a bit, but she finally got out, "Well... I don't know."

Just then, Olivia jumped in: "Look, if you wanna do this, I'll cover for you. You can say the three of us girls are going to the movies together."

Everyone mumbled their agreement, but Fatima struggled with the idea at first. Eventually, she gave in and said, "Okay, I'll try for you, Marcus, but I can't guarantee anything. I'll try my best though."

"Cool," Marcus said. He kissed her on the cheek.

Later that night, Marcus got a call from Olivia. "What's up?" he asked.

"It's on," Olivia said.

Excited, Marcus replied, "Are you for real?"

"Yup."

"Girl, I could kiss you," Marcus said.

Over the line, Olivia laughed. "Save all that for your girlfriend," she said.

"Thanks."

"You're welcome. That's what BFFs are for."

"True," Marcus answered. "So what's the plan? How we gonna do this?"

"Well, I just talked to Tim, and I guess the plan is Josette's gonna pick me up, then we'll pick up Fatima. Tim's gonna come and get you and then we'll all meet up at the theatre."

"Oh, you're going too?"

"Unfortunately, yes, 'cause I have to be there to pick up Fatima and it would take too much time to bring me all the way back home. It would majorly cut into your time with her, 'cause remember she can't be out all night," Olivia said. "Don't worry, I'll give you two your space, 'cause I don't wanna be around all that mushy stuff."

"I'm cool with it, sis," Marcus said.

Saturday finally rolled around. Tim was having breakfast with his parents when his dad asked, "So son, what are your plans for today?"

Tim responded, "I have a dinner and movie date with a special someone."

"Oh really?" His mom replied.

"Yup. I'm going to have dinner with her and her folks."

"Wow, she must really like you, son," Mr. Wilson said.

"We really like each other."

"Well, they better be nice to you," Mrs. Wilson said. "Or they'll have to deal with me!"

Tim laughed and said, "I'm sure they will, Mom."

"Son, always remember to be a gentleman, but I'm sure you already know this," his father said.

"I do. You and Mom have taught me well." This put a smile on both his parents' faces.

Later on that day, Tim called Josette with another idea for the double date. "Hey babe," he greeted, "Would you be cool if we just took your car to pick everybody up instead of taking two cars? It would save time and headaches."

"I thought you guys didn't want Fatima's parents to see you two," Josette said.

"We don't," Tim replied, "We'll jump out of the car around the corner from her house, then you can pick us back up on the way out."

"Okay," Josette said, "I know it was my idea for us to double date, but I wish it was just us going out."

"I know, babe," Tim said. "And next time, we will; we'll have a great time."

Josette sighed, so Tim added, "Babe, don't you believe in romance?"

"Of course I do," Josette replied.

"Those two really like each other and are fighting the odds to be together. Surely we can help them out just this one time?" Tim said.

"Okay, okay, but why does Olivia have to come? Why can't I just go pick Fatima up?"

"Babe, I told you before, because her parents know Olivia and trust her."

Frustrated, Josette replied, "Okay. You're lucky you're my soul mate."

"Yes, I am," Tim replied. "I'll see you at six o'clock."

"I can't wait!"

"Neither can I."

When six o'clock rolled around, Tim's doorbell rang. Tim was upstairs, in the final stages of preparation for the night, so his mother answered the door instead. "Well, hello young lady," she said.

Josette, being very polite, responded, "Good evening, Mrs. Wilson."

Mrs. Wilson then called over her husband, who had been relaxing on the couch. He came over and said hello, to which Josette replied, "Hello, sir."

Mr. Wilson smiled, then called up the stairs: "Wow, son, you've done well. She's very pretty."

Blushing, Josette replied, "Aww, thank you sir. I can see where Tim gets his good looks. No disrespect, Mrs. Shaw."

"None taken, young lady," Mrs. Wilson replied.

"Thank you," said Mr. Wilson. He then turned toward the stairs again and called, "Son, don't keep the pretty lady waiting for you!"

Tim ran down the stairs. A little bit out of breath but excited, he said, "Hey."

"Hey back at ya," Josette replied. "You look very handsome."

"Thanks, and you look very beautiful, as usual," Tim said.

With a big smile, Josette thanked her boyfriend. For a moment, they just looked into each other's eyes; Tim's parents watched them, then looked at each other and smiled. Eventually, though, Mr. Wilson cleared his throat.

"Um, son?" he started.

Tim caught himself and laughed. "You've met my parents already, I see?" he asked Josette.

"Yes, I have," she replied.

"Good. Well then, I guess we're off," Tim said. They all said their goodbyes and Mrs. Wilson invited Josette over for dinner sometime in the near future. Josette graciously accepted, and then out the door they went. The couple jumped in the car, and Josette wasted no time in giving Tim a nice soft kiss.

"I've been looking forward to that all day," she said.

"Wow. Me too," Tim answered.

"Your parents are really nice," said Josette. "Now I know why you're such a gentleman."

Right as she was about to start the car and drive off, Tim stopped her. "Wait, I forgot something," he said. His abruptness startled Josette, causing her to slam on the brakes.

"Tim!" she yelled.

"Sorry, but this is very important!" he replied.

"Okay, then hurry up," Josette said, giggling slightly.

"I'll be quick." He jumped out of the car and ran back into the house. Tim made a beeline straight up to his room.

His parents looked at each other in dismay, wondering why he was in such a panic.

"Tim, honey, is everything okay?" Mrs. Wilson called up to her son.

Just then, Tim came back down the stairs with a dozen roses, told his mom, "Everything's perfect," and gave her a kiss on the cheek. Once again, he was out the door and approaching the car, only this time with a bouquet hiding behind his back.

"So are you okay now?" Josette asked.

"Yes," Tim replied, "And these are for you." He pulled the flowers out from behind his back and handed them to his girlfriend. Josette gasped.

"Oh my, for me?" she asked, eyes wide and smile stretching from ear to ear.

"Yup."

Obviously overwhelmed, Josette said, "Oh, thank you! You're so sweet." She leaned in and gave her boyfriend a kiss. Both teenagers were unaware of Tim's parents watching them through the window to see how things would play out.

"Aww," cooed Mrs. Wilson.

"That's my boy."

"That he is, honey," Mrs. Wilson said, then she kissed her husband.

Meanwhile, back outside, Tim and Josette were ready to go. Josette tossed the keys to Tim. "You drive," she said.

"Okay," Tim agreed.

On the drive to Josette's house, Josette leaned her head on Tim's shoulder and sighed contentedly. Not many words were exchanged during the drive, but they didn't have to be. Sometimes silence is golden, and at that moment, being together was all that mattered to the couple.

Fifteen minutes later, they pulled up to Josette's house. "Well, here we are," she said.

Nervously, Tim replied, "Yeah, I guess we are. I really hope your parents like me."

"Trust me, they'll fall for you, just like I did."

"Is that right?"

"Uh-huh!" Josette giggled and brought her face closer to Tim's. Right as they were about to kiss, the front door of Josette's house swung open. Standing right in the doorway were her mom and dad, plus her 11 year-old brother, James.

"Eww!" yelled James. Quickly, the couple drew back from each other and got out of the car. They marched up to the front door, where Josette's mother was the first to greet them.

"We heard the car pull up and couldn't wait to meet

you," she said, and extended her hand to her daughter's boyfriend. "Hi, I'm Carol."

Tim took her hand, and then she proceeded to introduce him to the rest of the family. "Tim, this is my husband, Chris, and my son, James."

Looking at Tim in a reserved and cautious manner, Josette's dad shook his hand with a firm, kung-fu grip. Tim tried to laugh it off, saying, "Wow, sir, what a grip! You must work out."

"Oh yes. Hell, you never know when my daughter might bring a boy home and I'll have to throw him out on his head," Josette's father said.

Frustrated, Josette yelled, "Daddy!"

"Well, I'm just saying."

Mrs. Smith took this moment to jump into the conversation. "Chris! Mind your manners, dear." She turned to Tim. "Tim, you pay him no mind."

"It's okay, Mrs. Smith," Tim said, "If I had a beautiful and wonderful daughter like his, I'd be a little cautious, too."

Now it was time to shake James's hand. Right before Tim could extend his palm, he noticed that Josette's brother had a finger up his nose. Tim's face scrunched up a little, but he gave the child a small fist-bump instead.

"I'm sorry, where are my manners? Come on in," Mrs. Smith said.

"Thanks," Tim replied, and followed her and the others inside. He was in awe; the house was extravagant! Upon realizing this, it dawned on Tim that Mr. Smith must be pretty wealthy.

"Wow, what an amazing house. You must do very well for yourself, Mr. Smith," he said.

"I guess I do okay," Mr. Smith replied with a smug grin on his face. Mrs. Smith then requested for everyone to be seated in their grand living room.

Wow, I can't believe I couldn't see that her dad was loaded, Tim thought to himself. Next thing he knew, Mr. Smith was asking him what his parents did for a living.

"My dad is in real estate," Tim answered, "and my mom's an accountant."

"I see," Josette's father replied. Once again, his wife jumped into the conversation.

"Honey, can you help in the kitchen?" she called. Although he grumbled about it a little, Mr. Smith reluctantly stood up to join his wife.

"Don't be mean to Tim," she snapped at him. "I think he's a nice boy."

"I'm not being mean, just careful. She's my baby and she's been hurt enough." He frowned. "I just want to make sure he has the best intentions and isn't out to get something for nothing."

"I understand, honey, but you have to at least give the young man a chance and trust Josette. I think she's learned her lesson and wouldn't be bringing Tim here unless there was something special about him."

"Okay, okay," Mr. Smith said. "Now let's eat, I'm starving."

The two of them brought out the food and placed it on the table. "Wow," Tim said, "This looks great, Mrs. Smith."

"Thank you, Tim. I hope you like it."

"Oh, I'm sure I will."

On the table were plates of spaghetti and meatballs, garlic bread, Caesar salad, and freshly grated parmesan cheese. Right before they began to eat, Mrs. Smith asked Tim if he would say grace.

Despite being a little uncomfortable, Tim accepted. "Sure," he said, then bowed his head. "I'd like to thank God for the food we're about to receive, and Josette and the Smiths for having me over. Amen."

As soon as he finished, everyone dove right into their meals. After a minute or two, Mrs. Smith asked her daughter, "Sweetie, how did you two meet?"

"I've known Tim since tenth grade, and we've seen each other around school and in class," Josette responded.

"I've always liked her and wanted to ask her out, but she was seeing someone else most of that time," Tim added.

Then, out of the blue, Josette's little brother asked, "Are you gonna try to boink my sister?"

Tim choked on his garlic bread for a second. As he coughed and spluttered, Mrs. Smith raised her voice, *"James!"*

Suddenly, there was more tension at the table. Angered, Josette said, "James, you butthead!"

"Well, you didn't answer the question," Mr. Smith said.

"Sir, I highly respect your daughter," Tim responded slowly. "I've never even brought the topic up. This is actually the first time it's come up, so your answer is no."

Angrily, Josette stood up. "That's it," she growled. "Come on Tim, let's go. You don't deserve this."

Confused, Tim did as his girlfriend asked. But before they could leave, Mr. Smith said, "Wait, you both. Sit down. You're right, Josette, he doesn't deserve this." He turned to look Tim in the eye. "I want to apologize for me and my son. Tim, I love my little girl and I don't want to see her get hurt again."

The couple sat back down. Tim nodded and said, "I understand, but sir, I think she's wonderful too, so I would never hurt her. Right now, we're still in the getting-to-know-each-other stage."

"Fair enough," Mr. Smith said. The tension at the table seemed to have dissipated for the time being, so everyone moved on to discuss happier things like school and sports. An hour and a half had passed before Tim and Josette excused themselves from the dinner table so they could meet up with their friends.

"Thank you for having me, the food was amazing," Tim said to the Smiths.

"Thank you, Tim. I really hope you'll come again," Mrs. Smith said. Once again, Tim thanked her before heading out the door with Josette.

On the way to pick up the others, Josette had a worried look on her face. "I hope my family didn't turn you off," she said to Tim. "I'm really sorry for what happened."

"Babe, I'm fine. It'll take more than that to scare me away," replied Tim. "I'm here for the long haul. You're stuck with me, babe."

"You say that like it's a bad place to be." Josette laughed. "I'm glad we're stuck together." She gave him a quick kiss, but the moment was quickly interrupted when Tim's cell phone rang.

"You guys on your way here?" Marcus asked when Tim picked up.

"Yeah, we should be there in about twenty minutes," Tim replied.

"How was dinner with the folks?"

"Eventful."

"You can't really talk right now, can you?" Marcus asked.

"Nope."

"I feel you, we'll talk later."

"You know we will," Tim said, and hung up. Josette could tell what the conversation was about, but she just stayed quiet about it, smiling and holding Tim's hand tight in hers. He gave her hand a bit of a squeeze, giving her a look that said "I'm not going anywhere." She looked back at him and smiled, and the drive continued.

As they got closer to Marcus's home, Josette began to observe the changed surroundings. It was then that she realized they were on the shadier side of town. A little worried, she squeezed Tim's hand tightly. Recognizing the fear in her eyes, he squeezed back.

"Does Marcus live around here?" she asked.

"Yup, right around the corner."

"Oh."

"Don't worry," Tim reassured his girlfriend, "Nobody's gonna bother us."

"You sure?"

"Very sure."

"Okay, but I'm not getting out of the car."

Tim laughed. "We won't have to," he said. "Marcus is meeting us out in front of his house."

"Good."

Tim took out his cell phone and called Marcus to let him know they were close. Marcus gave them the okay and Tim hung up, only to pull up in front of Marcus's home five minutes later. There he was, waiting for them. Tim rolled down his window. "Jump in, buddy!" he called. Marcus did just that, throwing himself in the back seat.

"Hey, Josette," he greeted.

"Hello."

"Good looking out," he said to both of them. "Thanks for picking me up."

"That's what friends are for," Tim said.

Olivia's house was ten minutes away. Marcus texted her quickly to let her know they were a few minutes away and to meet them out front. She sent them an "ok" in reply. Not long after that, the group was pulling up in front of her place. As she approached the car, she and Josette exchanged chilly greetings, then she jumped in the back seat with Marcus. "You are soooo lucky you're my brother," she mumbled.

"You my dawg. Thanks, sis." Marcus laughed, then cleared his throat. "So how we gonna do this again?"

Olivia replied, "When we get around the corner from her house, you boys are gonna have to jump out and Josette and I will grab Fatima. Then we'll come back and get you two."

"Cool," said Marcus. "I called her after you texted me to

let her know we would be there in about half an hour or so."

While driving to Fatima's house, Marcus asked Tim how the mix was going for the demo they all did together.

"Good. I have it now; you wanna hear it?" Tim asked.

"Hell yeah!" Marcus said. "Put it on!"

Tim took the CD out of its case and put it into the player. After a minute or two, everyone was moving around and banging their heads to the beat. Olivia's vocals were spot-on.

"Man, that's tight!" Marcus said.

"Yeah, it's good! I really like it, Tim," Olivia agreed.

"Thanks," Tim replied. He turned to Josette. "So what do you think?"

"I think it's really good. I'm impressed!" she said, then turned to the back and added, "Olivia, you're really good."

"Thanks." It seemed to ease some of the tension between the two girls a little.

A few more minutes passed, then Olivia pointed to a spot nearby. "Tim, pull up over there," she said. They were just around the corner from Fatima's place. Once he did pull up, the boys jumped out of the car and let the girls continue on to Fatima's.

As they pulled up, they spotted Fatima outside waiting for them with her mom and dad. They all exchanged greetings and Mrs. Puja told them to have a good time. Mr. Puja was a bit stand-offish at first, but then gave his daughter a hug and said, "Don't stay out too late, okay?"

"Yes, I know, Daddy," Fatima replied, then turned around and got in the car with her friends. It was pretty obvious how excited she was about this event.

"I've never deceived my parents like this before, so I feel a little bad," she said. "But I'm excited at the same time."

"I love your parents too, and I'm a part of the conspiracy, but hey, you only live once and you're almost out of school! Plus, you're not doing anything wrong," Olivia said. They pulled back up to the boys and let them hop in the car.

When Marcus jumped in, he asked, "How you doing, beautiful?"

"I'm good," Fatima replied. "I'm feeling a little guilty about deceiving my parents, though. I've never lied to them before."

"I understand, but don't you think I'm worth it just this once?"

"Of course I do, otherwise I wouldn't be here!" Fatima replied. "But I love my parents too."

Marcus was obviously excited by this. "You said you love them too. Does that mean you love me?"

Fatima laughed. "Next topic!" she said, and everyone laughed.

"Well, I'm glad you're here," Marcus said.

"Me too," said Olivia.

"So are we," Tim added, referring to both himself and Josette.

During the drive to the movie they all laughed and joked around, singing songs on the radio and having a really good time. They decided to see a romantic comedy called *Da Gino*. At one point during the movie, Olivia looked at her friends all cuddled up with their girlfriends, and for a moment she felt alone. Tim caught this and stretched the arm that was around Josette over to Marcus so he could tap him on the shoulder. Marcus looked over at Tim to see what he wanted, but before anything could be communicated, he noticed Olivia. Fatima and Josette picked up on this as well.

Marcus nodded his head and put an arm around Olivia too. She smiled at him. "Thanks, Marcus, but I'm okay," she said.

"I didn't ask if you were okay, I just wanted to show my friend some love. Is that cool?"

She laughed. "Sure."

Fatima showed her approval by giving Marcus a quick kiss on the cheek and laying her head on his shoulder. A couple seats away, Josette did the same.

The movie ended at around ten, and Fatima only had an hour left before she had to be back home, so they all decided to go across the street to the Cheesecake Factory for dessert.

While eating their cheesecakes, everyone was laughing and having a good time; however, at one point, Tim noticed a beautiful woman staring at them out of the corner of his eye. She looked as if she were anywhere from 25 to 28. With his eyes, Tim got Marcus's attention and gestured for him to look to his left. Marcus did, and also noticed the lady looking their way. He looked at Tim, silently telling him "I see what you mean."

Ten minutes later, the mystery woman stood up to leave. Before she did, though, Tim noticed her talking to the waiter, and both of them looking in his direction. The waiter nodded his head. The woman smiled at Tim, then turned to leave the restaurant.

Josette looked at her watch and realized that Fatima didn't have much time left before she had to be back, so they all got up to go. Tim asked the waiter for the bill, but the waiter said that a young woman had already paid for them and left a note. Everyone was surprised by this.

Tim took the note and read it out loud:

"I love to see young people in love. Signed, Orenda."

Everyone thought the gesture was nice, but Tim couldn't help feeling a sense of unease and foreboding. He kept his thoughts to himself, however, and went on with the others to take Fatima home.

During the car ride, Marcus and Fatima held hands, the latter resting her head on Marcus's shoulder. They were silent while Olivia just gazed out the window. Nobody said very much until it was time for the boys to get out of the car again.

Just before the girls drove off again, Marcus walked up to the window on Fatima's side, leaned in, and gave her a big kiss.

"Dang, y'all, get a room!" Olivia said. Her comment made everyone laugh, while Marcus and Fatima pulled apart.

"Good night, baby," he said.

"Good night, my sweet prince," she replied. "I'll try to call you tomorrow."

"Cool."

The girls drove away to drop Fatima off. In the meantime, both Marcus and Tim began to joke around, Tim saying, "Man, you're whipped."

"Look who's talking," Marcus responded. "So are you!"

They both burst out laughing, but stopped when all of a sudden Marcus said, "Damn, I smell something burning."

"Me too," Tim replied. About thirty feet away, the boys spotted what looked to be moving smoke.

"Is that smoke?" Marcus asked.

"Yeah, I think it is," Tim replied. "But I don't see a fire. This is weird."

"Yeah it is."

Before the smoke got their full attention, Josette and Olivia drove up to them. "Hop in, boys," said Olivia. They did, but as they began to drive off, Tim and Marcus attempted to observe the smoke. Before they could, however, Josette looked to Tim in the passenger seat.

"Did you miss me?" she asked.

"But of course," Tim replied, tearing his eyes away from where he had been looking.

"Good."

Olivia rolled her eyes at this, then while acting like she had to cough, sneaked in a quick "Whipped," which made Marcus crack up with laughter.

Tim had heard them. "Yes," he snapped, "And I'm proud of it."

They all laughed. Olivia interrupted it quickly, though, saying, "Marcus, what you laughing for? You're just as bad."

"Yeah, but I'm cool with it," he replied. Once again, everyone started to laugh.

As they made their way home, nobody noticed a pair of eyes materialize within the plume of smoke Tim and Marcus had seen earlier. Soon after, a body followed—the body of the woman who had paid for their dessert. She stood with a menacing look on her face, watching the car drive away. She disappeared again in an instant, back within the smoke, dissolving into the night.

CHAPTER 6
The Legend of Wytobse

Tim and Josette dropped Marcus and Olivia off at their homes and made their way back to his place. Pulling into his driveway, she turned to him slowly—locking her eyes with his.

"Thank you for the awesome evening." Josette smiled.

"You just took the words right out of my mouth," Tim said, brushing her hair aside. "I guess great minds really do think alike." He leaned over and kissed her. He could feel her lips twisting into a smile.

"I love you," she said softly.

"You do?"

"Yes, I do, but I'm not expecting you to feel the same way or anything," she blurted, looking down at her lap.

Smiling, Tim gently lifted her face to his. "You're a few years late, sweetie. I've loved you since the tenth grade." He smiled.

She wrapped her arms around him, holding him tightly in her arms. "I had no idea, Tim, but I'm glad you still do," she said as she kissed him again.

Glancing outside, Tim was in awe of the beautiful full moon bestowed before them and its perfect light beaming down on them in the car. From the corner of his eye, he saw the time on the dashboard clock. Realizing that Josette needed to get home before her curfew, he said, "I better let you get home before it gets much later."

She nodded and stepped out of the car, leaving Tim with a final kiss goodnight. She drove off, leaving Tim smiling his driveway.

Careful not to wake his family, Tim quietly tiptoed to his room in the dark, fumbling to maintain his footing. As he reached his room, he slowly opened the door and noticed the fluorescent light from his computer screen was flashing in the dark. Flipping on the light, he walked over to his desk and flopped onto his bed, staring at his computer. It was an e-mail from Professor Waters.

Tim, I'm so sorry it's taken so long for me to get back to you. I finally spoke to the Chief today, who had some surprising news. From what I've shown and told him, he thinks that you, Marcus, and Olivia may be in grave danger. He wants to meet all three of you and see the items for himself. Are you and the others available to meet next Saturday? Let me know ASAP.

Signed, Mitch Waters

Without hesitation, Tim quickly replied to his e-mail.

Dear Professor,

Thank you for writing back to me. I'll talk to the others tomorrow and get back to you immediately after.

Tim

Confused and worried by the abruptness of the professor's message, Tim began to wonder about the intensity of the objects. Had they stumbled upon something sacred, or worse yet, illegal? Before his worries could take over, he noticed a new e-mail pop up on his screen. It was from Josette.

Tim,

I just wanted you to know I had a great time tonight and how wonderful I think you are. I love you, Tim.

Josette

P.S. Sorry for the way my dad and little brother acted. You handled it perfectly and I truly admire that.

He turned off his computer and made way to his bed, turning off his light. As he lay in the dark, he closed his eyes and listened intently to the silence around him. Visions of his future with Josette began to dance across his mind, and the news from the professor seemed like a faint memory as he fell into a deep sleep.

Starting to dream, Tim envisioned himself walking to the top of a steep hill. He looked below him to see hundreds of angry Native warriors lead by a mysterious figure. The figure looked up at Tim with an icy stare.

"You have something of mine," he said.

With his words, the warriors behind him begin to throw hundreds of spears, tomahawks, and knives at Tim. He knew these people wanted something from him. He knew they would kill him to get it. He closed his eyes to escape the battle, and when he opened them again, corpses were littered across the land. Amongst the groans of pain, he heard a sobbing from behind him. Turning to the noise, Tim came face to face with a young boy. Appearing to be in his early teens, the boy was sobbing with his head held in hands. Realizing that Tim was staring at him, the boy looked directly into his eyes, causing a sudden feeling of sadness to wash over him. It was not until the boy turned to walk away that Tim noticed he was holding the staff in his hand.

Tim bolted up at the sound of his alarm clock. Despite the cool breeze coming in from the window, his clothes were drenched in sweat. He got out of bed and walked to the window, wiping the sweat off of his forehead. Hearing his mother calling for him from the kitchen, he suddenly realized how hungry he was. He quickly changed into a fresh set of clothes and headed down to the kitchen to find his mother at the table.

"Where's Dad?"

His mother placed a luscious plate of French toast, scrambled eggs, and bacon in front of him. "He went to go play golf this morning, dear."

Immediately, Tim dove into his breakfast, heading for the bacon first.

"How was your date last night, son?"

"It was great," he said, crunching down on the sweet bacon.

"That's good. How were her parents? Were they nice to you?" his mother asked.

Tim swallowed his chewed food. "Her mom was really nice, but her dad and little brother were a bit of a challenge at first. It all worked out in the end, though."

Mrs. Wilson laughed. "Well, you know how fathers are with their daughters. You're a great person, Tim. They'll warm up to you in time."

"I sure hope so, Mom," he replied.

After breakfast, Tim went back to his room and to his computer, where he suddenly remembered about the e-mail from Professor Waters. He noticed both Olivia and Marcus were on Skype and called them immediately.

"Hey guys, I got an e-mail from the professor last night and it was kind of weird. He wants us all to go meet that chief guy with him next weekend. He said we might be in danger."

"No shit," replied Marcus. "The shit that happened in the woods that last time made that quite clear."

Olivia replied, "We've had nothing but trouble since we found this stuff. I told you it was cursed! We all need to pray."

Tim shuffled in his seat. "What we need to do is find out what we have and why somebody would kill for it. Let's meet up with the professor on the weekend and find out what to do next."

"All right, fine," Marcus and Olivia agreed. "We should also agree to keep this on the down low until we meet with the professor."

Tim nodded. "Okay, it's between us three only, then. I'll see you all soon."

By the time Monday had come, Tim and Marcus were still on cloud nine from their weekend dates. The next week was their senior prom and the group of had plenty of plans to make. It was lunch hour and they were all seated at their usual table.

"To think we only have a few more weeks of high school and that our prom is next week! Are you guys as excited as I am?" asked Josette.

Everyone except Olivia nodded in agreement.

"I don't really care much about prom, but I'll go anyway," she said, taking a sip of her Coke. "Fatima, did you talk to your parents about going to prom yet?"

"I spoke to my mom and she's okay with it, but I haven't talked to my dad yet. I think my mom is going to talk to him for me, but I think I'll be able to go when it's all said and done," replied Fatima.

"I sure hope you can go!" chimed in Marcus. "My night won't be the same without you there."

Fatima smiled and placed her hand on Marcus's. "That's so sweet, Marcus."

"Yeah, sweet like Ricky Martin," snorted Olivia. The group of friends burst into laughter before their laughs were drowned out but the sound of the bell.

The week passed by unusually fast—much to the delight of Tim and his friends. It was Friday night and Tim was watching a movie in his living room when Professor Waters called him to remind him of their meeting. They agreed that the professor would pick them up early on Saturday morning and that they would bring the artefacts. Before he hung up the phone, Professor Waters warned Tim to be cautious. After the call, Tim contacted Olivia and Marcus and told them the plan.

As promised, Professor Waters arrived at Tim's house early in the morning the next day. Hiding the staff in his guitar case, Tim jumped into the car. He noticed the professor had a deep look of concern on his face.

"I would say good morning, but the look on your face tells me otherwise."

Professor Waters replied, "To be honest, I don't know what is going on, but the chief told me that if the artefacts are what he believes they are, not only are you, Marcus, and Olivia in grave danger, but mankind is, as well."

Tim stared at the professor in disbelief, too shocked to say anything. "That's what I'm told. I'll find out if it's true when the rest of you find out."

They proceeded to pick up the others. As Marcus and Olivia got into the car, they could both sense that something was not right.

"So Professor, what's up?" asked Marcus.

"I'm not sure," Professor Waters said. "It seems these items you have are worth more than any of us have known and that there are some people out there who would kill to have them."

Nervous, Olivia chimed in, "We should all pray, because maybe we disturbed something by taking these items."

The professor shook his head. "I don't know what the deal is, but we'll all find out soon enough. The chief seemed really concerned and wanted to meet with us right away. I've known him for a long time and I've never known him to be so worried."

The children shuffled, uncomfortable in their seats.

"So brace yourselves, kids," he continued. "We might be in for a wild ride."

The three hour drive to Chief Ahote's reserve was a silent trip, as everyone seemed to be in deep thought.

"We're here, kids," Professor Waters said, breaking the silence.

"Where exactly is 'here'?" Marcus replied skeptically.

"Wenacee," responded the professor. "The chief is part of the Watnomi tribe. We have thirty minutes to hike to the reserve."

"Oh great," Marcus groaned.

They started hiking and walked until they came to a sign that read:

The Watnomi people welcome you.

They walked up to the chief's house, which resembled a cozy cabin from the outside. Professor Waters knocked on the door while the children waited on the steps. After a few moments, the chief—an elderly man with an aged, wrinkled face—greeted the group and welcomed them into his home.

"Welcome, my friends. I am Chief Ahote. Please come in and make yourselves comfortable."

As they entered the house, they were immediately taken aback with all of the marvellous artefacts in the home. There were ancient Native items ranging from weapons to carvings, headpieces, and rugs. It felt as if the children had gone through a time warp to the past.

The chief, however, did not waste any time concerning the artefacts and asked to see them almost immediately. First, Olivia presented the wolf's hide. Chief Ahote took it into his hands rubbed the fur between his fingers.

"Yes, this is the hide of the mystical Silver Wolf. It is said that those who wear his hide can become of his likeness."

Olivia sat wide-eyed in amazement as Marcus showed Chief Ahote the feathered crown. He scanned the different feathers that lined the crown and handed it back to Marcus.

"This is the mystical feather crown. Legend has it that anyone in possession of this crown can change into different birds that are represented by each feather in the crown." They all looked at each other in amazement.

Chief Ahote paused for a second and turned to Tim. "So Tim, let me see what you have there in your guitar case."

Slowly, Tim unzipped the case and pulled out the staff. Amazed, the chief looked at it and said, "So the legend is true. I can't believe it."

Confused, Professor Waters cut in: "Sorry, what can't you believe, Chief?"

"He holds Wytobse—the staff of the four winds!" Chief Ahote exclaimed, lifting his hands into the air.

Professor Waters sat back in his chair and stared in disbelief. "Now I understand why those men came after you kids. I understand why Justin Sigo wanted this so bad."

Chief Ahote shot a glance at the professor. "Did you just say Justin Sigo?"

The professor nodded. "Do you know him?"

Without replying, Chief Ahote stood up and left the room, leaving the group confused. When he returned, he held an old book covered with dust.

"Let me tell you a story," he said. "Back in the eighteen hundreds, an evil shaman started a war with his tribe because he was filled with greed and jealousy of wanting the power of Wytobse to himself."

The Chief told them of a young shaman who was given

the staff and how he alone, with its power, managed to kill thousands of their people. This young shaman eventually became a great chief and was revealed to be Chief Ahote's great grandfather. The professor and the others listened intently to his story, staring in disbelief at the man in front of them.

The chief continued his story, explaining that Justin Sigo was a descendant of the evil shaman. "Like me, Justin probably thought the mysteries of the staff were just a myth until he came across you." Chief Ahote closed the book. "And now, I believe he will stop at nothing to get it."

The room was quiet, with only the sounds of the chirping birds outside to be heard.

Tim broke the silence. "So what do we do now?"

Chief Ahote looked over at Tim and frowned. "What you will have to do will not be easy. Before this, I thought that the staff was a myth too, but now I think it may be real. If it is, there is a journey you will have to take, and grave dangers may be involved." He then pulled out an old map and laid it across the table in front of them, pointing to a remote area.

"You will have to take the staff and the other items here. The legend says it is a sacred ground with a cave in the mountains where the spirits of the great Chiefs dwell. They will protect the staff and the other items from evil." He rolled up the map and handed it to Professor Waters. "Have there been any incidents since finding the items?"

Marcus laughed. "Well, I kind of turned into a bird."

"And I turned into a wolf. I was *still* cute," Olivia replied with a smirk. Marcus rolled his eyes.

"I've been having these weird dreams about the war you just told us about, Chief," Tim said. "There are thousands of Native warriors charging toward this hill and I'm standing at the top. There's someone else there too; a young boy who is crying. I can only see his face but I can tell he's a teenager. Then I turn to look back at the warriors. Instead, I see devastation and death everywhere. Then I turn to look at the boy, but he's already turned and walking away." He took a breath. "It all seems so real that I wake up in a cold sweat. I know this boy is trying to tell me something, but I just can't put the pieces together."

The chief, who was listening intently, put his hand on Tim's shoulder.

"Tim, I think his spirit lives within the staff. He's trying to show you the immense power you have in your hands and how dangerous it could be in the wrong ones."

"Chief, how are Justin and his men able to change into things too?" Olivia asked.

Chief Ahote sighed and sat back down in his chair. "Because, like you, they have found powerful objects. Justin is also a shaman, which means he can cast spells and conjure magic. We have suspected that he is a part of a group of evil shamans that practice the dark arts. Now, from what you tell us, we know for sure he is." The children looked at each other, amazed. "This is not good, but I believe you three were chosen for this—especially you, Tim."

Tim felt a sudden wave of responsibility weigh down on his shoulders as he realized what this meant.

"Let me speak with the other shamans and I will contact you all soon with a plan." He turned to Tim and the others. "In the meantime, I want to give you all this symbol of the great wolf spirit to protect you for now. Take the items with you and keep them hidden. May the Creator protect you."

On that note, the meeting was adjourned. After they collected their items and bid the chief farewell, the group began the hike back down the professor's car in silence. They were all trying to take everything in that Chief Ahote had just told them. The drive back to the city was silent except for Professor Waters warning the trio to be on alert.

Marcus, the first one to be delivered home, received a text message from Fatima as soon as he stepped out of the car. She was allowed to go to the prom next weekend. Marcus was beaming with excitement and almost forgot the situation he was in until he remembered he was holding the feathered crown in his bag. The feelings of excitement quickly vanished as he hurried into his house.

Professor Waters then dropped Olivia off at home. She immediately went into her bedroom and knelt at the foot of her bed to pray. She asked God to protect her and her friends through this troubled time and whatever they may face in the future.

By then, Tim was almost home and still in the car with the professor. "I'm scared, Professor," he said. "I'm scared and worried about myself and all of us."

"No matter what happens, I'll be by your side the entire time, Tim. Don't worry. We'll fight this together," he assured.

Hearing the professor's words provided comfort for Tim, who thanked Professor Waters for his care.

Once Tim arrived home, he immediately went upstairs to hide the staff. Keeping it in the guitar case, he placed it on the floor of his closet under a few shirts and sweaters. Pleased with his stash, he got up and turned on his computer to check his e-mail. While reading through a few chain e-mails, he continued to glance over at the guitar case in his closet. Finally, after a few minutes, curiosity got the best of him and he rushed over to the case. Lifting it from under his clothes, he carried it over to his bed and unzipped it. He pulled out the staff, eyeing it curiously and wondering how something like this could have so much power. Observing the staff closely, he examined the talisman tied around it.

Noting the fine features, Tim went to his computer to access Google and search the significance of the symbol. He came across a picture of the exact symbol on the talisman. Underneath the image were the words 'The Four Winds.'

"So that's what it means," he said to himself quietly. He fiddled with the staff in his hands and held it out in front of him.

"So how do you work?" he asked. "Let's see here… Alah Kazam!"

Nothing.

He tried again. "Make wind!"

After a few futile attempts, Tim finally gave up and put the staff back into the guitar case. "I'll figure you out one day."

He placed the case back into the closet and hid it under his clothes. His attention was then drawn to his computer, which was beeping. He glanced over and saw that it was Josette calling him on Skype. He jumped up and rushed over to his computer to answer her call. They began to chat, but Tim's mind was elsewhere—on the staff.

"Hello handsome," she said sweetly.

"Hey, babe," he answered.

During their conversation, Josette could tell that something was on Tim's mind.

"Are you all right, Tim? You seem sort of upset."

He replied, "I'm just thinking about life after school, and how everything is going to change."

"I understand," she said. "It's a lot to think about. I'll come by tomorrow and we can take a walk and talk a bit."

Tim smiled. "That would be great. How's one in the afternoon work for you?"

"That sounds great. I better get going, so I'll see you tomorrow. Bye, Tim!"

Following his chat with Josette, Tim decided to do some research on Native history and myths. As he started to read different articles and stories, he came across a story about the great staff and how it had the power to conjure up hurricane-force winds in the blink of an eye. It read that the staff was a gift from the spirits of nature and only the pure of heart may control its power. It spoke of the Great War that Chief Ahote described and how its power was unleashed on thousands of Native warriors who had tried to obtain its power. After the incident, the staff was never seen again and no one was ever brave enough to try to steal it. The whole land mourned for years after.

Tim, in utter disbelief, began to wonder if this story was actually a myth or if there was some truth to it. Maybe Professor Waters and Chief Ahote were just pulling his leg and playing a prank on him. But at the same time, Tim knew what he had seen back in the woods.

He typed "Justin Sigo" into Google to find out more about him. There was a biography page dedicated to Justin, detailing his entire life story from his birth to how he became a millionaire and an important figure in the community. There were many write-ups about him and about the artefacts he owned. Tim could feel his head start to hurt from staring at the computer screen for so long and retired from his computer. He picked up his guitar and began to strum a tune.

At this same time across the city, unbeknownst to Tim, Marcus was playing his keyboard and Olivia was sitting on her back porch singing and playing her guitar. As ironic as it seemed, it was truly not, for all three of them drew strength from their music. It was something the trio shared.

CHAPTER 7
Prom Time

Finally, the day of the prom had arrived, and everyone was excited when they met up that morning. Josette was the last to arrive, and when she came up to Tim, she hugged him from behind.

"Are you ready for tonight?" She smiled at him.

"I sure am," he replied.

"Good, because I'm going to make myself look extra beautiful for you."

"Babe, I don't think you can get more beautiful than you are now."

"Aw, you're so sweet, Tim!" Josette said as she kissed him. "I'm really excited for tonight."

"So am I," Marcus said as he held Fatima's hand. Tim asked Olivia if she was excited for prom.

She replied, "Not really, but I'll be there."

Fatima jumped in and said, "We'll be there together, my friend."

"Well, the only reason I'm even going is cause of you guys," Olivia said.

Marcus chimed in, "Well, I got selfish reasons for why

I'm glad you're going."

"Well, what could those be?" Tim asked.

They all pointed to Josette and laughed.

"So what's the plan with Fatima?" Tim asked. "My dad rented a limo for us and it's going to pick everyone up. It's going to pick Marcus and Olivia first, so you two may have to play each other's date. Then it's going to pick up Josette and me and off we'll go to the prom! On the way back, it'll drop everyone off at home."

Marcus nodded. "Sounds like a plan."

Since it was the day of the prom, all of the seniors were allowed to leave early to have time to get ready. Since the prom started at 8:00 PM, they had plenty of time to dress up. Marcus was the first one to be picked up by the limo. He looked very dapper with his black tuxedo, pink shirt, and black bowtie. As he walked over to the limo with a rose in hand, his family and even some neighbors outside cheered him on. The next stop was Olivia's house. It seemed as if her whole family was there. Her mom was crying tears of joy and beaming with pride. Marcus didn't see Olivia at first, but Olivia's mom quickly called her out of the house.

"Hurry, Olivia, the limo is here!" her mother called. Olivia stepped out of the house. Marcus had to do a double take at the beautiful girl who was walking toward the limo. He always thought she was cute, but he had never seen her look like this. She had always been a bit of a tomboy and dressed down with glasses and her hair up. Marcus sat in the limo, stunned. As she climbed inside, Olivia's mom whispered to her sister.

"Look at Marcus's face!" she giggled. They all laughed as they waved goodbye.

On their way to Fatima's house, Marcus was still sitting in disbelief, staring at Olivia. Noticing his stare, she asked, "Boy, what are you looking at? Stop staring at me!"

"Who are you?" Marcus asked.

Olivia laughed. "I can play dress up when I want to, silly."

He nodded in agreement. "No shit."

Flattered, she laughed and quickly changed the topic. "So are you excited to see Fatima?"

"Most definitely," he said.

"If I must say, you're looking very pretty dapper yourself. I think she will be pleased when she sees you."

He smiled. "I know, it's cause I'm bringing sexy back!"

She laughed said, "God, you're so stupid."

"Nope, just confident."

"Whatever, player." Olivia sighed and shook her head.

Twenty minutes passed until they had arrived at Fatima's house. Marcus was nervous and excited at the same time. As they pulled up, Olivia called Fatima to let them know they had arrived. About five minutes passed before Fatima appeared at the front door looking stunning, but with her parents in tow. Olivia jumped out of the limo to greet her and say hello to her folks. Fatima looked at Olivia and said, "Wow, look how beautiful you are!"

"You're one to talk girl, you're stunning!" Olivia replied. They giggled and hugged while Olivia greeted her parents. Fatima's dad seemed a bit distracted.

"Who's the guy in the limo?" he asked.

Olivia replied, "Oh he's just a friend. He's with me."

With a very curious look on his face, he looked on at Marcus. "Oh, all right."

Mrs. Puja ushered them into the limo so they wouldn't be late. Fatima kissed her mother and father on the cheek, which made them smile. The girls ran to the limo and jumped in. Fatima's folks waved goodbye. Once in the limo, Fatima looked over at Marcus with a big smile. The look on his face said it all.

"You look beautiful, baby."

"Thank you, Marcus! You look quite handsome yourself." Fatima smiled.

"Thanks, babe. Oh, I have something for you," he said as he handed her a long-stemmed red rose he had been hiding behind his back.

She smiled and said, "Thank you, my prince."

"You're welcome, my Queen," he said. She gave him a peck on the cheek, and the two of them took their seats, ready to pick up the others, starting with Tim.

When the limo pulled up to his house, Tim came out looking dashing with a black tuxedo on. As he moved over to the limo, he looked at Olivia and asked, "Wow, what happened to you?"

She rolled her eyes. "Whatever."

"You're gorgeous!" he exclaimed.

"Thank you," she said softly as her face turned red.

"Marcus, man, you sure clean up good. And Fatima, you look beautiful as well!"

They both thanked him, then headed off to pick up Josette. When they arrived at her house, Josette's brother was out on the porch with a couple of his friends doing tricks on their skateboards. When he saw the limo pulling up, he called out to his sister that they had arrived. Tim jumped out of the limo and walked up to the door. Before he could knock, Mrs. Smith opened the door.

"My, you look handsome tonight, Tim," she said. "Josette will be down in a moment."

Her father came out from the living room. "I want her back at a decent hour, son. I trust you'll be a gentleman with her tonight, if you know what I mean."

Tim straightened his back and smiled. "Yes, sir, I do

know what you mean and I will always be a respectful gentleman with her, I promise."

As he finished talking, Josette appeared at the top of the staircase in a stunning blue dress and began to walk toward Tim. Tim's eyes filled with delight as a huge grin spread across his face. Just as she made it to the bottom of the stairs, Tim pulled a dozen pink roses out from behind his back. He handed them to her and told her she looked beautiful. Before she could answer, her father blurted out, "Damn right she does."

Mrs. Smith rolled her eyes. Meanwhile, Josette ignored her father's outburst and said, "Thank you Tim, you look quite handsome yourself."

In response to her husband's outburst, Mrs. Smith blurted out, "Damn right he does." He looked at her and laughed.

"Okay, okay, I was just saying."

"Sure you were, dear. So was I. Now you two run off and have a good time." she said.

"Not too good a time." Mr. Smith added.

Tim smiled. "Don't worry, sir, it'll be just like you at your prom."

As the headed off to the limo, Josette's mother laughed.

"Honey, didn't you get lucky at your prom?" She laughed again, covering her mouth to stifle the giggles.

In a nervous tone, he said as he began to walk away, "I

don't want to talk about it."

Once in the limo, Josette saw Olivia first and gasped in amazement. "Oh my, you're gorgeous!"

Everyone burst out laughing. "What's so funny?" she asked.

"That's what we all said," they laughed. Olivia rolled her eyes and smiled.

"I mean, you all look nice, but you really caught me off-guard," Josette said shyly.

"Thank you, but can we change the topic now?" said Olivia.

"All right, we'll leave it alone." Tim said.

"Hey, don't hate us because we think you're beautiful!" Marcus laughed.

Once they arrived at the prom, everyone had the same reaction when they saw Olivia. The students all gasped and stared as she made her entrance, but there was one guy in particular who was dumbstruck at Olivia. His name was Nathan Stevens. He had always had a crush on her but was always too afraid to ask her out. Seeing her tonight made his heart sink. He had been confident that tonight would be the night he would break the ice and ask her out, but now he was even more afraid to ask. She and Nathan were both 'A' students and would sometimes study together. Olivia sort of knew that he liked her because she had caught him staring at her more than once. Though she thought it was cute, she only viewed Nathan as a friend. Josette's friends saw them coming in and immediately stole her away.

"Sorry, Tim, but we have to steal our girl for a little while," said one of her friends.

"Steal away." Tim smiled.

"Are you sure?" Josette asked.

"I am. Go have fun with your friends," he replied.

She kissed him on the cheek. "Well, try not to miss me too much."

He laughed. "It's too late for that!"

She kissed him again as she ran off with her friends, giddy and excited, and didn't notice that her ex-boyfriend saw her kiss Tim. Although he was there with a date, his ego couldn't handle the view. One of his friends tapped him on the shoulder. "Hey Shawn, it looks like your ex has moved on, man," he said.

Shawn replied, "Good for her." He looked at his date and said, "I know I have."

Meanwhile, Olivia saw Nathan standing alone and walked over to him.

"Hey Nathan," she said in a nervous tone.

He replied, "Oh, hey, Olivia. You look amazing tonight. Not that you don't any other time, I mean you look great then too, but –"

"Thank you." She cut him off. "So did you bring a date?"

"No, I came alone," he said. "Did you?"

"Nope, I came with my friends," she replied. "Did you want to hang out with us?"

Nathan smiled. "Sure, that would be cool."

She walked him over to where everyone was standing, and they all greeted him with a friendly hello. Marcus moved close to Olivia and whispered in her ear, "You know you just made this boy's night, right?"

"Shut up, man!" she hissed. Marcus laughed.

"Hey, I'm going to grab a drink. Can I get you one, too?" Nathan asked, standing up.

"Sure," Olivia said.

"I'll grab you one too, babe," Marcus said to Fatima.

Marcus grabbed Tim and Nathan. "Let's go boys, the women are thirsty!"

As the three walked over to the refreshment table, Tim made a pit stop over to Josette to let her know he was getting a drink for her. She thanked him and he continued on to the bar. Just as he turned around, Josette's ex and his friends approached Tim.

"Well, Tim, how does it feel to have my sloppy seconds?" Shawn smirked. "You're a fool if you believe everything she tells you."

His friends laughed, but Shawn did not. Everybody started to notice the confrontation going on and started to converge. Olivia and Fatima were there first, followed by Josette and her cheerleader friends.

"You're a fool for not knowing what a good woman you had until it was too late," Tim replied. "But I won't make that same mistake, so don't hate, masturbate."

Shawn was starting to get really angry and pushed through his friends to get right up to Tim's face. Even though Shawn was bigger than him, Tim did not back down. Instead, he pushed Shawn back and began to go at him, coming nose to nose with him again. Just then, Marcus appeared behind Tim with a few of his friends from the basketball team. "Don't start none, won't be none," he said firmly.

"You can't fucking talk to me like this," Shawn said angrily.

"Then don't come up to me saying some sloppy seconds garbage about my girlfriend when you know you never got further than a kiss."

At first, Josette was beaming with pride to see her man protecting her until she heart the 'sloppy seconds' comment. That was when she jumped in.

"SLOPPY SECONDS?" she yelled. "You never got close

to hitting this! You even tried to get me to touch it and I almost threw up at the thought! The only thing sloppy about our so-called relationship was your kisses and I'm sure your date knows what I'm talking about."

Shawn's date snickered a bit and then put on a straight face. Beyond embarrassed, he asked his date, "Do you think I'm a sloppy kisser?"

She didn't answer and looked off to the side. Shawn then said, "Whatever, you two deserve each other."

Josette said, "Shawn, that's the only thing you've said tonight that makes sense."

Defeated, he walked off in a huff with his crew behind him. Everyone around them laughed and Tim continued on to the bar. Josette turned to Tim and gave him a big hug and kiss for standing up for her. Not five minutes later, the DJ was playing a slow song—an old tune called "Always and Forever." Tim asked Josette to dance and lead her to the dance floor. At the same time, Marcus had been doing the same thing with Fatima, leaving Olivia and Nathan standing there. Nathan wanted to ask Olivia to dance, but he was too terrified. On the dance floor, Tim and Marcus were enjoying their dances with the loves of their lives, but Marcus couldn't help but notice Olivia and Nathan standing there, so Marcus whispered to Tim, "Hey check out those two. Let's get them on the dance floor."

They got Olivia's attention and began to gesture her to dance with Nathan. Out of sight of Nathan, she gestured back she did not want to. Then, several guys started coming up to her and asking her to dance or if they could get her something to eat or drink. She said no to all of them. Some of them even went as far as to ask for her phone number. All of this amused Marcus and Tim, who could see it all unfolding, and knowing their friend well enough to know how uncomfortable all the attention was making her feel. Finally, Olivia had enough and grabbed Nathan's hand and led him to the dance floor.

"Let's do this," she said to him. Assuming Nathan didn't know how to dance, she toned her dancing down a bit.

After a few minutes, Nathan said, "You know I can dance, right?"

"Oh, really?" Olivia laughed.

"Yes, so if you want to let loose, don't hold back. I think I can keep up."

With a chuckle, Olivia said, "You sure?"

"Very," Nathan replied.

At that moment, a very popular hip-hop song came on. That got everyone excited and more people came on to the dance floor. Olivia went into her dance routine; she was very good. Marcus, Tim, and the others looked on, but before they could feel bad for Nathan, he started to bust out his own moves. Everyone stared with their mouths open. Nathan could really dance, and he was doing more than holding his own with Olivia. Shocked, Marcus looked over at Tim.

"Can you believe this? Who would have known!" he said.

"I know, it's awesome!" Tim laughed. The crowd formed a circle around the two. They shone together in the spotlight. Olivia and Nathan came to the prom expecting a night where they would both have a lousy time, but it had turned out to be the time of their lives. This set the tone for the rest of the night. They had a great time. At the end of the night, everyone waited outside for the limo to pick them up. No one wanted the night to end, but Fatima had to be home at a certain time. Before they got into the limo, Marcus grabbed Fatima and pulled her to him.

"This might be my last chance to do this tonight," he said as he gave her a big squeeze. "I just want you to know that being here right now with you has been the highlight of my life. Thank you for making tonight so special."

Tearing up, Fatima smiled. "I feel the same way and I couldn't have said it more perfectly." She touched the side of his face and kissed him one more time. Then, they all jumped into the limo, where Tim and Josette were already cuddled up. Josette whispered to Tim, "Thank you for being my hero tonight."

"Your days of relationship drama are over, I promise," Tim said.

"I know. I feel safe with you." She smiled as she leaned over and pressed her lips to his.

Meanwhile, Olivia was looking out the window. She was

happy she had come, but was feeling a little alone seeing her friends in love. A part of her wished she had someone, too.

Fatima got dropped off first, and right before they pulled up to her house, knowing she couldn't bring the roses in with her, she cut off a rose with a little bit of stem and put it into her purse.

"I want something to remind me of you and this night," she said. She squeezed Marcus's hand before she got out of the limo to meet her parents at the front door.

Mrs. Puja embraced her daughter. Seeing how happy Fatima was made her happy, too. She turned and waved goodbye to everyone, then off they went. Next, they went to drop off Marcus and Olivia. In the end, it was just Tim and Josette in the limo. On the way to drop off Josette, Tim said, "Tonight was perfect."

Josette replied, "You mean even with all my ex drama?"

Tim laughed. "Well yes, he stepped out of line and someone had to pull him back in his place and we both did that."

"I must admit, you looked sexy standing up for me," Josette teased.

"He needed to understand that you're my girlfriend. He blew it."

"See, that's why I love you, Tim." She leaned in to kiss him when all of a sudden the limo driver suddenly slammed on the breaks, causing both Tim and Josette to fall forward.

The limo driver got out in a panic and ran to the front of the car, thinking he had hit someone. There was nothing there except fog. He ran to the back of the limo to check on Tim and Josette. As they started to pick themselves off the limo floor, Tim looked around.

"What the hell was that?"

"I don't know, maybe he almost hit a deer." Josette replied. Suddenly, there was a tap on the window. Tim rolled it down to see the panicked limo driver.

"What happened?" Tim asked.

"I'm so sorry kids, I thought someone walked in front of the limo. It's so foggy out here. Maybe I'm seeing things. Once again, I'm sorry."

"It's okay, we're fine." Tim said, even though they were shaken up a bit. As they drove away, a shadowy figure watched them amid the fog.

Soon enough, around 11:45, the limo arrived at Josette's house, where her parents had waited up for her. As soon as the limo pulled up, Tim gave her another smooch. Her parents greeted her at the door and waved goodbye to Tim. As the limo pulled out, Mr. Smith yelled, "A gentleman would have walked her to the door!"

"Daddy, stop, please don't ruin my night." Josette frowned.

"I'm not, I'm just –"

"Enough dear," Mrs. Smith cut in. "Now tell me all about your night, Josette."

Tim made it home without any more obstructions. Tired from the night, he passed out on the bed in the clothes he wore to prom. He liked to leave his window cracked for air, but on this particular night, he should have closed it. Outside his window was a patch of fog that began to seep into his room through the window crack. It came in and slid across the floor, where it transformed into a person: the beautiful woman from the Cheesecake Factory. She looked around Tim's room and walked up to him sleeping on the bed. She leaned over him and whispered, "I could kill you right now. You're lucky Justin won't let me."

The smoky fumes coming off her body gave Tim a bit of a cough, so she backed up from him. She looked around the room again, and stopped at the closet. Something inside her told her it was there—Justin's prize. She then slowly began to approach the closet. In his sleep, Tim started to mumble a chant. Just as she went to reach out for the door handle, a sudden gust of wind threw her backward with a great force. Before she slammed into the wall, she changed into the same misty form she had used to enter the room, emitting a faint wail.

Tim woke up in a cold sweat from the sound of the scream. He got up to close his window, thinking maybe it was the whistling wind that he heard. On the ground outside his window, a very frustrated and confused woman, who didn't fear most things, stood alone. Tonight had been a bit of a fright for the woman. Angry, she stood for a few minutes in her human form before changing back to the mist and flying on. Tim went back to sleep.

Later, the mystery woman made a call to Justin.

"We will have to be more careful. I just felt its power," she said.

"I don't want you getting too close, Orenda. I just want you to observe and be patient. We will get the staff soon, my friend. Very soon."

CHAPTER 8
Grad and Beyond

*G*rad was a week away. Around the school, there was a somber feeling among the teachers and students. For the teachers, it was sad to see the students that they had moulded move on to uncertainty, and for the students, the fear of the unknown and splitting up with their friends of the last few years troubled them. Tim, Marcus, Olivia, Josette, and Fatima were all having a rough time with the thought of their group breaking up. Tim and Marcus were especially sad at the thought of having to be separated from Josette and Fatima. They hoped they could make their relationships work from a distance, and the girls felt the same. None of them knew what the future held, and it worried them all.

It was Monday afternoon when they all met up at lunch. Everyone at the table was thinking it, but Marcus was the first one to say anything. "So, Olivia, what happened to the swan?"

Olivia responded, "She's retired; that was a one-night only occasion. Getting glammed up is not my thing; this is the me I'm comfortable with."

Tim said, "Hey, fair enough. You'll always be our friend, no matter how you look."

"Yeah," Marcus agreed.

Blushing, Olivia said, "Thanks guys. It's gonna be really hard not seeing the crew after grad."

"I know, that's why I'm trying not to think about it too much," Tim responded. At that moment, a boy walked up to their table and greeted Olivia, telling her how amazing she looked at the prom. She thanked him, but then a few more walked by and said hello.

"Damn, O," Marcus said. "You done let the genie out of the bottle now. Everybody tryin' to holla at you!" He laughed.

"Whatever," Olivia replied, "I'm not interested and I don't need the attention."

Tim said, "Well, you got it now, sister. Bask in the glory."

"Yeah, own it!" Marcus said. Everyone at the table laughed, but then the bell rang and they all made their way back to class.

Later that night, Tim had another dream. This one was more intense than the last ones: he was running from something chasing him. He came to a cliff and was forced to either jump off it or face his fear of the thing behind him. He chose to fling himself off the cliff. As he fell backward, he could see the boy with the staff standing on the edge of the cliff. He called out, "Do not fear your fear. Fight it. You and your friends' lives will depend on it."

Tim woke up panting, his heart racing. He sat up in his

bed and wiped the sweat off his forehead, wondering what his dream meant. After a while, he eventually fell back to a deep slumber that didn't stop until morning.

The next day while everyone was at school, Mrs. Puja had been let off from work early and decided she would straighten up the house while everyone was gone. When she got to Fatima's room, she went to pick up some books off her bed and noticed what looked like a green stem peeking out from underneath the pillow. She pulled the pillow back and found a short-stemmed red rose. Mrs. Puja paused for a second and pondered if Fatima had been keeping a secret from her and her husband. She then continued to make up the bed and placed the rose back under the pillow where she found it.

When Fatima came home that afternoon, she gave her mom a kiss on the cheek and said, "Hello Mom, how was your day?"

"It was okay. I got in a bit early and cleaned the house," she replied.

"Oh, okay," said Fatima, unaware that her mother had been in her room. "Well Mom, I have some studying to do. Call me when dinner's ready, okay?"

"I will," said Mrs. Puja, but stopped Fatima right before she could dart up the stairs. "Wait, come talk to me for a second," she said.

A little surprised, Fatima responded, "Um, okay Mom. Is everything okay?"

"Oh, yes, yes," she replied. "We just haven't really talked much lately and I just wanted to catch up a bit. Is anything new going on in your life?"

"Not really," Fatima answered. "Just school and homework; you know, the usual."

"Oh, okay. Well I don't want to keep you from your schoolwork. I just wanted to check in and see how things were in your world."

"Well, things are great, thanks for asking, Mom." Fatima gave her mom a hug and headed up the stairs, feeling a bit uneasy about the exchange. Mrs. Puja was saddened by the conversation, and still felt Fatima was hiding something from her. In the past, that never would have been a factor because they were so close.

Feeling a bit worried, Fatima entered her room to find it was tidied up. She gasped and thought, *Oh my God, the rose*. Remembering she had left it under her pillow and seeing the bed made, she worried that it was gone, so she ran over to it and threw the pillow back. There it was, right where she had left it. She let out a little sigh of relief, but at the same time began to panic, thinking about how her mom had been acting earlier. She knew her mother had discovered the rose and that her daughter had been lying. Now Fatima knew that at some point she was going to have to tell her parents about her and Marcus.

A few hours passed. Mrs. Puja called everyone down for dinner, where things seemed normal, aside from Mrs. Puja being quieter than usual. After dinner, she went out to the front porch while her husband went down to his basement/media room to catch up on his sports. After a few minutes, Fatima went outside to join her mom. She sat down next to her on the swing-chair and they swung together in silence. After a few minutes had passed, Mrs. Puja said, "I remember you and I swinging here when you were a little girl, but now you're not a little kid anymore. You're a young woman and I have to accept this fact."

"I know, Mom. But like you said, I'm not a kid anymore, and soon I'll be on my own and have to take care of and think for myself. But you'll always be my mommy and I'll always be your little girl." Fatima wrapped her arms around her mom and laid her head on her shoulder. Then she said, "Mom, I know you saw the rose."

"Yes I did," she responded.

"Why didn't you ask me about it?"

"Because I thought I should wait until you were ready to tell me about it. Though I must say I'm a little surprised—you've never kept secrets from me before, so I was a little hurt that you would now."

"Mom, I'm so sorry if I hurt you," Fatima replied. "That was never my intention. I was so confused, and I've never felt this way about someone before and I just didn't want to disappoint you and Dad."

"You could never disappoint me, sweetie. I've always been so proud of you and I always will be. Please don't ever forget that!"

"Thanks, Mom," said a sobbing Fatima. "I won't forget. And I'm sorry I didn't tell you about him."

Her mom proceeded to give her a big motherly hug and said, "I may not always agree with you and your choices, but I'll always listen and I'll always be there for you. Now, I want to know about this young man you've been keeping secret from us."

Fatima replied, "Mom, he's wonderful, and he's a senior, too."

"How long have you been seeing him?" Mrs. Puja asked.

"Well, kinda right after the senior trip, but we've known each other for long before that."

"Is he a Muslim?"

Fatima paused for a second, then slowly replied, "No, he's not."

"Oh... I see. Do you really like him?"

"Mom, I love him, and he loves me, too," Fatima replied.

"Oh my," said Mrs. Puja. "I don't know what to say."

"Say you're happy that I'm happy."

"Well of course I am. I only want the best for you," Mrs. Puja said. "But remember, this is all new to me and I am a little surprised, but I want you to be happy. To be honest, I don't know how your father will take this, but I'll leave it up to you to tell him when you feel ready."

"Thank you, Mom," Fatima said. "Don't worry, I'll tell him no matter what."

The next day at school, Fatima walked up to Marcus and said in a serious tone, "Marcus, we need to talk."

Seeing the worried look on her face, he replied, "Sure, what's up?"

"My mom knows about us."

"How?" Marcus replied.

"She was cleaning my room and found one of the roses you gave me."

"Oh snap," Marcus responded. "What did she say?"

"Well, she was a little disappointed that I felt I couldn't talk to her and that you weren't Muslim, but she says she wants me to be happy," Fatima said.

"Do you think she's gonna tell your dad?"

Fatima replied, "No. She said she would leave it up to me, but she also said she didn't know how he'd react."

"Wow," said Marcus, "So what're you gonna do?"

She replied, "I'm scared, but I have to tell him sooner rather than later!"

"I understand and I'm here for you," Marcus said.

"I know you are," replied Fatima, then she gave him a big hug. As they embraced, Marcus asked, "What if your father forbids you to see me?"

Fatima replied, "I don't even want to think about that. I'll just have to convince him otherwise."

"I'll just have to cross my fingers and pray for a miracle."

At lunch time Marcus, Olivia and Tim made a plan to meet up at Tim's place after school to work on some music together, so they met in front of the school when the bell rang and jumped into Tim's car. Now that basketball season was over, Marcus had more time to jam with the others.

They jammed together for about two hours, then wrapped it up for the evening and decided to chat for a bit. Marcus started, saying, "I got news for y'all. I just found this out and I want y'all to be the first to know: I was offered a full basketball scholarship. Actually I was offered a few, and I'm really thinkin' about doing it, but I don't know if I wanna stay close or go far. I kinda wanna be close to Fatima."

"Well, find out where she's going and decide from there," Tim suggested.

"Aww, that's sweet," Olivia said. "She told me she was thinking of going to UCLA. She got a scholarship from there for pre-med."

A very excited Marcus responded, "Are you serious?! That was one of the places that offered me a scholarship!"

"Well there you go, now all you have to do is find out if she's gonna go there," Tim said.

"No time like the present," Olivia added. So she called Fatima on her cell phone. "Hey girl, what you doing?" She asked.

"Just studying," responded Fatima. "What are you up to?"

"I'm just working on some music with the boys," Olivia replied. "Hey, I was wondering if you decided what college you're gonna attend in the fall?"

"I've talked to my parents and they both think UCLA is a good bet because of their medical program. Where are you thinking of going?"

"Girl, I'm still on the fence," Olivia responded.

"Are you excited for this weekend?" Fatima asks.

"Yeah, but kinda sad as well. Hey, but I might have a surprise for you. Guess who else got a scholarship to UCLA?"

"Who? You?"

"Marcus! He was offered a basketball scholarship there

and a few other places."

Enthusiastically, Fatima replied, "Oh really? What's he gonna do?"

"Well he wants to stay close to you, but he hasn't discussed it with his family yet."

"I understand, but I hope he goes there."

"Me too."

Fatima then said, "Hey, my mom's calling me for dinner. I'll talk to you later. Tell Tim hello and give Marcus a kiss and a hug for me."

With a chuckle, Olivia replied, "Hun, I think I'll let you do that when you see him next."

Fatima laughed too, then said, "Fair enough. Bye!" and got off the phone.

"Later girl." Olivia hung up too.

"What did she say?" Marcus asked.

"She said she's going to UCLA and was excited you might be going there too. And to give you a hug and a kiss, which I declined," Olivia replied.

"Wow," Marcus said. "I got a lot to think about."

"Yes, you do," Olivia responded.

Mrs. Wilson invited them for dinner, but they all declined because their parents had dinner waiting for them at home, which Tim's mother understood. That meant it was time for Tim to take them home.

During the drive home, Tim told his friends about his latest crazy dream.

"What do you think this all means?" Olivia asked.

"I really don't know," Tim replied, "But something's trying to tell me something."

"Man, that's some wild shit," Marcus said.

"Yeah, creepy," Olivia agreed.

Soon they were at Olivia's place, dropping her off. Next was Marcus, but five minutes after Tim dropped his friend off, he realized Marcus left his lyric book in the back seat, so he called him up on his cell to tell him he was turning around to bring it back, and that he would call again when he got there. Five minutes later, he was calling Marcus to let him know he was waiting. As Tim sat there, two men watched and approached the car.

On his way out the door, Marcus looked out his window to see where the car was. He saw the men approaching Tim's car and knew it could be bad. "Oh shit!" he yelled, then ran as fast as he could.

One of the guys walked over to Tim's passenger side while the other walked over to the driver's side and said, "Hey man, I got that weed, I got that coke, whatcha need?"

"Thanks, but I'm good," Tim said.

Then the other guy said, "Okay, cool. By the way, I like this car." While distracted, the first guy pulled out a gun and smashed the passenger side's window with it. As Tim turned in shock toward the broken window, the man on the driver's side pulled out a gun as well and yelled at him to get out of the car. Just then, Marcus ran up to the car and threw himself at the would-be carjacker and Tim.

Marcus realized the carjackers were childhood friends of his; he recognized them by their voices and one of their jackets. With tension high, Marcus yelled, "Man what are you doing, he's a friend of mine!"

The jacker replied, "I don't care if he's a friend of yours, this cracker doesn't belong in this neighborhood. Now move, Marcus, or you can get shot with him."

"Then you're gonna have to shoot me, 'cause I'm not leaving my friend."

"So you'd die for this cracker?"

"Yup, just like I would've done for you back in the day."

Both carjackers looked at each other for a second, almost as if to reflect on a time when this would be true. They gave each other a nod and put their guns away. As they start to walk away, the one that was on the driver's side said, "White boy, you're lucky to be alive, and Marcus, you'd better be giving us some free basketball tickets when you go pro, 'cause you owe us."

"I got you," Marcus replied, and the two guys faded into

the darkness. Marcus turned back to Tim and asked, "Hey, you all right, man?"

"I guess, considering," Tim said.

"Hey man, I'm really sorry about all this," Marcus said.

"It's okay man, it's not your fault," Tim said. "Plus, you saved my life. I knew you were a great friend, but now I really know how great you are. Thank you."

"You don't have to thank me, that's what real friends do."

"You're right," Tim responded.

"What about your window? What are you gonna tell your folks?" Marcus asked.

"I'll make something up," replied Tim. "I can replace a window, but I can't replace my life. But, my friend, I'm gonna get out of here before I have any other bad breaks. Oh, and let's keep this between us; I don't want to worry anyone."

Marcus agreed and Tim went home. When he got there, he told his parents that someone broke the window when he stopped at Marcus's place for a minute. Needless to say, they forbade him from driving around that area at night anymore.

Finally the big day had arrived: graduation day. There was excitement in the air and a sense of pride and accomplishment all around, as well as a bit of sadness. Lots of faculty and family members were waiting around on school grounds for the ceremony to begin. Some parents already had tears trickling down their faces, while some beamed with pride for their sons and daughters.

It was a beautiful June day, so the ceremony was being held outside on the field. Marcus was with his mom, grandmother, and siblings. Tim was there with his parents, and they came with Fatima's. Josette was with her parents and younger brother in tow. Excited to see each other, the friends all gathered for a minute to greet each other's families.

When Fatima introduced Marcus to her parents, there was almost a nervousness in the transaction. Mrs. Puja caught Tim and Olivia giving each other a glance and put two and two together: this must have been the young man Fatima spoke of.

"Mom and Dad," Fatima started, "This is Marcus."

Marcus shook Mr. Puja's hand. "Hello, sir," he said.

"Hello," Mr. Puja responded.

Marcus shook Mrs. Puja's hand and said, "Hello, Mrs. Puja."

She shook his hand firmly and looked him in the eyes, saying, "Very nice to meet you, young man."

Marcus, Tim and Fatima all looked at each other, then Mrs. Puja embraced her daughter and said in her ear, "He seems like a nice young man."

Fatima responded, "Mom, he really is, but how did you know?"

Her mom answered, "Sweetie, mothers always know. Now go graduate."

At that moment, the students and parents were called to take their seats so the proceedings could begin. Tim, Olivia, Marcus, Fatima and Josette all sat together, with Tim next to Josette and Marcus next to Fatima. The commencement was set up on the football field with the students sitting on chairs set up for the grad ceremony, and the families sitting on bleachers to watch the proceedings.

The grad ceremony was around three hours long, and at one point during the proceedings, Mr. Puja, armed with a pair of binoculars to watch the ceremony, went to focus in on his daughter. As he focused in he noticed she was holding Marcus's hand. He jumped out of his seat and yelled, "What the hell?" which disrupted the ceremony for the moment. That prompted his wife to pull him back down to his seat.

"What's wrong with you?" she asked.

Angrily, he responded, "Fatima's holding that Marcus guy's hand. I saw it with my binoculars."

"Honey, don't you dare ruin our daughter's big day. She doesn't deserve that," Mrs. Puja said. "You can talk to her later about this, but not now. This is her day and she and I won't speak to you for a long time if you do."

The other parents were visibly upset by the outburst and Mr. Puja could see the embarrassment in his daughter's face, so he calmed down and gathered his composure while the ceremony continued.

"What's up with your dad?" Marcus asked Fatima.

"I think he knows about us now," she replied.

"Are you okay?" Marcus asked. Fatima gave his hand a squeeze and looked into his eyes. "I've never been better," she said.

Being valedictorian, Fatima had to give a speech for the class, but at one point in her speech, she looked up to where her parents were seated, as if to address them directly. "I want to thank my Mom and Dad for always being there for me and supporting me and trusting me to make decisions for myself," she said. Those words seemed to really hit home with her father, who knew he could be a little overbearing, but thought he was only doing what was best for his daughter. He realized now that he could have lightened up a bit, and started to tear up along with his wife. He knew in his heart that he and his wife raised an amazing young woman and he would have to let go.

After the ceremony, the students took pictures together with faculty and their families. When Fatima's parents approached her, she went to start apologizing to her dad. He cut her off instead and said, "Look, we can discuss this later, but right now I just want you to know how so very proud we are of you."

She teared up and gave her dad an enormous hug and said in his ear, "I love you too Daddy, you're the best." That brought the three of them to tears, and a group hug ensued among them all.

Marcus, Tim, and Olivia walked over to the family just then, and Marcus asked if he could join the group hug. Mr. Puja said, "I'm not there yet," which made everyone laugh. A little embarrassed, Marcus said, "Oookay."

Off in the distance, the woman that had paid for the kids' desserts watched the ceremony as well. "Aww, so cute. Enjoy it while you can, young ones," she whispered to herself, then disappeared in a cloud of smoke.

Later that night, there were several grad parties going on. One of the bigger ones was at Josette's place. Tim picked up Olivia, Marcus and—surprisingly—Fatima, who had the blessing of both her parents to attend. Josette's parents and little brother stayed away for the night so that Josette could have time alone for the party.

The party itself was going great; everyone was having a good time. Meanwhile at the reservation, however, Chief Ahote got a surprise visit. He walked into his house and his wife approached him, saying, "There's someone here to see you, dear."

In his living room, very tall and dressed in black, stood Justin Sigo. Surprised, the chief's eyes grew big and filled with anger. "What are you doing here, Justin?" he asked.

"That's no way to address a fellow tribesman. I'm here for business," Justin replied.

"What kind of business could you possibly have with me?"

"I'm trying to get my hands on an ancient staff, and I know you know how I can get it," Justin answered calmly.

"I don't know about any staff," Chief Ahote responded. Justin stepped over to the table and picked up a book that was left there.

"This looks like an interesting story," he said. "What's it about? A staff that can control the winds? I have the same book; go figure. I guess great minds think alike."

Chief Ahote responded, "No, we don't think alike. Your thoughts are evil and mine are pure."

"Evil?" Justin replied. "I'm not evil, I just want to take back what was stolen from us. I thought you, for sure, would understand that, Chief."

"Of course I can understand the frustration among my people, but there are ways to address the issue without hurting others in the process."

"You and the others are fools if you believe this, and I intend to make it right by any means necessary," Justin responded. "Now, back to business. If you can obtain the staff for me, I will pay you one million dollars. Surely you could use that money, Chief. Think of the things you and your family could do."

In an angry tone, Chief Ahote replied, "Like I said, I don't know anything about a staff."

Suddenly, Justin's calm demeanour started to change, and he said furiously, "I will have that staff!"

Then, right before the chief, Justin's eyes turned black and his voice took on an eerie tone. He approached the chief, cornering him, and said, "I might have saved you before, but now you've become one of them to me."

Chief Ahote's eyes grew wide as he realized he was staring right into the face of evil. All of a sudden, the front door flew open and another young man walked in. "Chief," he said, "I'm feeling a negative presence on the reservation." The young man stopped in his tracks, feeling the negative energy increase in strength. It was strongest around Justin, as that was where the energy was radiating from. He could hear the chief's heart rate beating off the chairs and asked, "Are you okay, Chief? Sorry for barging in, but I had to talk to you."

"I'm okay," he replied. "Justin was just leaving. Isn't that right, Justin?"

"Oh yes," Justin said. "But you will see me again, old man, and circumstances will be different next time." He looked at the young man with a smile on his face as he walked out the door.

Relieved, Chief Ahote exhaled deeply. The young man asked, "Who was he, Chief?"

"Big trouble, son. Big trouble."

He quickly picked up the phone and called Professor Waters, leaving a message for him to call back as soon as possible.

Outside, after leaving the reservation, Justin walked away. Materializing next to him was Orenda. "Did you find anything?" he asked her. While he had been talking to the chief, Orenda had entered the house through an open window in her mist state and looked around.

"I saw something interesting," she said to Justin. "A map to the Island of the Ancients."

"Hmm. Now why would that just be lying around?" Justin asked. He took a minute to think and said, "Unless someone was planning on paying a visit there with a certain relic."

"But why take it there?" Orenda asked.

"Because the power of the spirits there would protect it, and we can't let that happen, now can we?" Justin replied.

"No, we can't."

"We need to get everyone together and join them on their quest," Justin said. "We'll lay low for now and get them in the forest."

Orenda agreed, then the two of them hopped into Justin's car and drove off into the night.

CHAPTER 9
The Quest Begins

Three days after Chief Ahote had been visited by Justin, he finally heard back from Professor Waters, who had been on a dig when the message had been sent. He hadn't heard the message until he had gotten home. When he called Ahote, Professor Waters didn't hesitate to ask what was going on.

"The kids are in great danger," the chief told his friend over the phone. "I need to speak with all of you right away. What I must tell you cannot be said over the phone."

"All right. I'll let them know." Professor Waters hung up the phone, then sat down in his chair for a moment before picking it back up to dial Tim's number. Tim didn't pick up, so the professor just left a message telling him to call back as soon as possible. He did a few hours later.

"Hey, Professor. You called?"

"Yes," Professor Waters answered. Tim could tell by the shakiness of his voice that something wasn't right.

"What's the problem?" he asked.

"Chief Ahote wants to speak to us. He called me and it sounded urgent, so we have to meet him as soon as possible."

"Okay, I'll get the others ready." Within minutes, Tim had hung up with the professor and called up Marcus and

Olivia. They all agreed to go with the professor early the next day.

At ten the next morning, Professor Waters picked up Tim, Olivia, and Marcus to take them to Chief Ahote's home. When they got there, they were rushed inside. "Sorry, but the forest has eyes and ears," he apologized.

"It's okay," Tim said, but he exchanged worried and bewildered glances with Marcus, Olivia, and Professor Waters anyway. There was another man standing by the chief, and he put a kind of powder under the door. Upon closer inspection, the guests found that every other door and window had similar substances between their cracks, and there were various Native symbols and pictures scattered throughout the room.

"What is all this?" Olivia asked.

"It's to ward off evil," answered the man next to the chief. "It's to make sure that no outside forces can hear this conversation or come in here. And by the way," he added, "My name is Peter."

"Peter is a practicing shaman here at the reservation," Chief Ahote explained. "He sensed an evil presence in Justin Sigo, who just showed up here asking questions about the staff. There was something very menacing about the whole visit and I feel that you all are in very great danger. He will stop at nothing to get that staff, and if it can do as the legends claim, then the whole world is at stake."

"So what's next?" the professor asked.

"It has to go to the Cave of the Ancients, and you must move on this quickly before Justin realizes what we are doing."

Panic began to fill the eyes of the four of them as they looked back and forth among each other.

"This is deep," Marcus said.

"Is this the only way?" Olivia asked.

Peter nodded. "Evil will find these artefacts if we don't protect them. This is the only way we can do that. I will personally accompany you as a guide on your journey."

"I suggest you all tell your parents you'll be going away for a while. Tell them I'm taking you on a dig for the next two weeks," said Professor Waters. Everyone agreed to do it and to get back to him as soon as possible.

That night, after talking with his parents, Tim called Professor Waters and told him everything was okay to go, not only for him, but Marcus and Olivia as well.

"All right," Professor Waters said. "I'll get all our camping gear and pick you up the morning after tomorrow, around five o'clock. Just relay the plan to the others and rest up until then."

Tim agreed, then made a quick call to Josette, asking her to go out with him the next day. He wanted to spend his last night with her before they both left, since he knew she would be going on a cruise with her family soon as well.

"So would that be okay?" he asked once everything had been explained.

"Of course," Josette replied. "I can't wait to see you. Good night!"

"Night."

Tim picked up Josette the next day and drove her to the local lake. They took a walk near the water's edge and held hands, swinging them and just enjoying one another's company.

"I'm really going to miss you this summer," Josette said.

"I'm gonna miss you too, but we'll both be back in time to spend some time together before we start school," Tim replied.

"You really think we can make it through school together?"

"I don't know, but I'm sure as hell gonna try." Tim squeezed her hand. "Why, don't you think we can?"

"I think that if two people really want to be together, they'll find a way," Josette said with a smile.

"Me too," Tim agreed. "But let's not think about that right now; I don't want anything to ruin this moment with you here and now."

"I agree." Josette put a hand around his waist and leaned her head on his shoulder and sighed. Tim swung an arm around her shoulder as they continued walking, forgetting about what the future may hold for them both.

After he had settled everything with his parents, Marcus got a call from Fatima. She explained that her parents wanted to invite him over for dinner the night before he left. Knowing how important this was to her, but still apprehensive, Marcus reluctantly agreed to go. Since he didn't have a car, his mother agreed to drive Marcus to Fatima's house. On the way there, she said, "So, you really like this girl, don't you, son?"

"Yeah Mom, I do."

"Well, she seemed like a nice girl from that brief moment we met her at your graduation. And since you're meeting her parents tonight, I assume the feelings you have for her are mutual?"

"Yup."

"Well, son," she said, "If you're happy, then I'm happy for you. You're a wonderful young man and I'm sure her parents will see this."

"Thanks, Mom."

"And if they don't, that's their loss," she added.

Marcus mumbled "Yeah, I guess," in agreement, but he secretly hoped that wouldn't be the case. The rest of the drive was quiet until they neared her house. It was a very large, lavish place with a perfectly-groomed landscape. Marcus and his mother both looked at each other in awe.

"Wow, this is a nice place," she said.

"Yeah, it really is." Marcus had never gotten to see her house on the night of the prom, since his relationship with Fatima had still been a secret from her parents then.

He got out of the car after saying a quick goodbye to his mother and made his way to the front door. Marcus was incredibly nervous about meeting his girlfriend's parents, but nonetheless, he found himself standing outside her house, armed with flowers, and ringing the doorbell.

Marcus could hear footsteps rushing toward the door just after the chime of the bell died down. Seconds later, Fatima appeared, throwing the door open with a huge grin on her face. She gave him a quick hug, keeping it short as if to show respect to her parents, who were watching from the background. When she released him, Marcus walked over to greet Fatima's parents, first extending a hand to her father. He shook Marcus's hand with a death-grip of a handshake. Getting the message, Marcus moved on to Fatima's mother. She gave him a warm hug. "Welcome to our home," she greeted. "Please, come in."

"You have a lovely home," Marcus said, looking around

the house.

"Why thank you, Marcus," she replied.

"Yes, we have worked hard to afford this," Mr. Puja said. "Do you know what I mean, Marcus?"

"Yes, sir, I do," Marcus replied. Mr. Puja gestured for Marcus to follow him. When he did, Fatima hung back for a second to turn around and give her mother a kiss on the cheek.

"Thanks, Mom," she whispered.

"For what, dear?"

"Just for being wonderful you."

Mrs. Puja laughed and hugged her daughter, then pointed ahead of them to Marcus, who was listening to her husband speak. "You should pay attention to him, sweetie," she told her daughter.

"Yes, I know." Fatima laughed a little bit, then hurried over to Marcus's side. When she reached him, she whispered quickly, "My mom likes you."

"Good," Marcus said. "That's one down, and one hard one to go."

Fatima's father continued the quick tour of the house with Marcus, showing him each room individually. Each space was even nicer than the last. The final room Marcus was shown to the dining room, where they would be eating. Mrs. Puja gestured toward the table.

"Now, you boys have a seat at the table. Fatima and I will serve you in a minute; I know you must be hungry," she said. Obediently, Marcus moved to the table with Fatima's father while the girls headed into the kitchen. There was an awkward silence at first, but soon enough, Mr. Puja chose to break it.

"So Marcus, what are your intentions with my daughter?"

Marcus swallowed nervously, not having expected that question. "Well, sir, I, uh..." But before he could answer, he was cut off once more.

"Look, she is not a loose girl. She is smart, classy, and responsible, so if you're only looking for someone for fun, she is not the girl you're looking for."

Marcus opened his mouth to speak again, a little indignant, but once again he was interrupted before he could get any words out. This time, it was with the arrival of Fatima, her mother, and the dinner they had made. "I hope you boys are good and hungry, because we have lots of food," Mrs. Puja said kindly. She and Fatima set the food down on the table, and as soon as they looked up they could feel a kind of tension in the air. The women looked at each other uneasily, then looked at Marcus. "Marcus, are you all right?"

"I'll be okay," Marcus replied, voice a little bit lower than usual. "But I have to say this, and with all due respect, Mr. Puja, all those things you said about your daughter are exactly why I care about her like I do. I'm not looking for anything other than respect, and sir; believe it or not, I'm a decent person, too."

"Yes, we will see," Mr. Puja replied. Fatima and her mother looked back and forth from the two men to each other, stunned.

"What happened here?" Mrs. Puja asked.

"I was just letting this young man know that our daughter is classy and responsible, and not a plaything,» her husband answered calmly.

"Dad!" Fatima blurted out in frustration. "Dad, he is *nothing* like that! He has only shown me the utmost respect! How can you judge him before you even know him?»

"She's right, dear!" Mrs. Puja chimed in. "The whole purpose of this dinner was to get to know him better, not to interrogate him!"

"Okay, okay, I get your point," Mr. Puja said. That was the end of that conversation, as right after he spoke, Mrs. Puja announced that it was time to eat. Grateful for the distraction, everyone tucked right into their meals.

Mrs. Puja had prepared a meal of Indian and African food. There were plates of naan, butter chicken, curry goat, rice, and vegetables. Marcus began to load his plate up with the steaming hot food when Mrs. Puja asked, "Marcus, have you ever had Indian food before?"

"Only butter chicken," he responded. "But this all looks and smells so good, I can't wait to get at it."

Mrs. Puja laughed. "Well, we wouldn't want to make you suffer any longer, now, would we? So let's eat." She bowed her head, followed by Fatima and Mr. Puja, so Marcus did the same. The family of three began to say a prayer, and when they were finished, it was on with the feast.

During dinner, Mrs. Puja asked, "So Marcus, do you and your family have any plans for the summer?"

"No big plans for the family, but I am going camping with some friends tomorrow."

"Oh, that sounds like fun."

"Marcus," interrupted Mr. Puja again, "What does your father do for a living?"

Marcus shifted uncomfortably in his seat. "I don't know, sir," he said. "I haven't seen him since I was a little kid. He abandoned us."

"I'm sorry to hear that," Mr. Puja said solemnly.

Not wanting anyone to pity him, Marcus shrugged. "It's all good. My mom and grandparents did a good job of raising us."

"We can see that," Mrs. Puja said. Her words seemed to lighten the somber tone somewhat. Moving on from that conversation, Fatima's mother then asked, "Where are you planning on going in the fall?"

"Well ma'am, first I was planning to go to Berklee School of Music for their recording engineering program, but I also got some scholarships to different schools, so I think I'm gonna go with UCLA on a basketball scholarship. I hear they have a pretty good music program, too."

"Wow, that's the same school Fatima is going to!" Mrs. Puja said. "And on a basketball scholarship, too. Did you know Fatima's father loves basketball as well?"

Mr. Puja was silent for a few moments, not acknowledging his wife's statement. Instead, he changed the subject, saying, "We are a Muslim family, Marcus. What do you think about the Muslim faith?"

"Well, sir, from what I know, it's a beautiful religion, despite how they talk about it on TV. But if I'm being honest, I respect everyone's freedom of religion, and I ain't one to judge," Marcus replied.

"Would you ever consider becoming Muslim?"

Marcus was a little bit surprised by the question, but answered anyway. "Right here and now I can't say, but I'd like to know more about the faith so I can honor Fatima."

Mrs. Puja grinned in approval, while her daughter couldn't fight back a radiant smile. This silenced Mr. Puja for the moment as he stewed over Marcus's answer. This gave Marcus a chance to ask his own questions about the family he was sharing dinner with.

"Mr. Puja, can I ask you a question?" Marcus started.

"Sure," answered Mr. Puja.

"Why are you so strict with Fatima?"

Everyone stopped moving; Fatima and her mother looked at each other quickly, then down at their plates. The question left an uncomfortable silence that stretched out for about ten seconds before Mr. Puja answered slowly, "Well, Marcus, I don't know if my daughter told you this, but... I lost my son in the war in our country before we came to live here." Marcus looked down at his plate, silent for a moment, while Mr. Puja continued. "I love my daughter with all of my heart and it would kill me to lose her, too. I only want the best for her."

Somber, Marcus nodded and replied quietly, "I understand, sir. I'm sorry for your loss."

"Thank you, Marcus," Mrs. Puja said. Her eyes had welled up with tears, along with Fatima's. But her daughter quickly wiped her eyes and changed the subject.

"So, Marcus... My dad's favorite basketball team is the Spurs. What's yours?"

He looked up, a little surprised by the sudden shift in conversation. "Oh? Mine is Miami," he said.

"Do you think they'll take it all?" asked Fatima's father.

"Yes sir. We've got LeBron."

"Well, they'll have to go through us first!" Mr. Puja insisted.

"Then I guess that's what they're gonna do!"

The two let out a big laugh and tucked back into their meals. After, Mr. Puja looked at his wife. "Is dessert ready?" he asked.

"Yes! Coming right up, dear," Mrs. Puja replied as she stood up. Fatima helped her mother to clear the table and wash the dishes while Mr. Puja asked Marcus to follow him into the basement. Inside was a small bar facing an enormous flat-screen TV and entertainment system. There happened to be a pro basketball game playing at the time, so the two men sat down to watch it.

Upstairs, the women were chatting away in the kitchen, unaware of where the men were hiding away. Fatima took a dish and rinsed it off, then brought a towel to it. As she dried the plate, she looked at her mom and asked, "So, what do you think?"

Mrs. Puja smiled. "I really like Marcus," she said. "I'm very happy for you."

Excited, Fatima thanked her mother and wrapped her arms around her. After a few seconds she suddenly pulled back to ask, "What about Dad?"

"Well, sweetie, he's a hard one to figure out, so I don't know how he feels," Mrs. Puja said. Fatima pouted, and her mother embraced her. "It'll be okay," she said. "Just give him a little bit more time to take it all in. This is a first for him and you're his world."

"I know, Mom."

"Now come on, we have to go back. They've been alone for too long now and we might have to referee them again."

Fatima chuckled. "Yeah, you're right."

When they stepped out of the kitchen and back into the dining room, both ladies were surprised to find that the room was empty. They began to panic slightly, and looked at each other to ask where the boys could have possibly gone, but their unspoken questions were answered with loud cheers coming from the basement. They made their way to the stairs and peered down. They could hear the men were excited from the game they were watching, and smiled at each other.

"This is good," Mrs. Puja told her daughter. "He ever takes anyone down who that isn't his close friend." Fatima laughed and jumped into the air, then nearly tackled her mother with a warm, loving hug.

"Mom, I'm so happy!" Fatima exclaimed.

"And I'm happy for you too, sweetie."

Before long, the sound of the doorbell was ringing throughout the house: Marcus's mother had arrived to pick him up. "Hello, Ms. Avery," Fatima said.

"It's nice to see you again," added Mrs. Puja.

"It's nice to see you, too," Marcus's mother replied. "My goodness, this is a lovely home."

"Thank you," replied Mrs. Puja. Just then, the boys came up from the basement. Marcus greeted his mother and went to her side, while Mr. Puja moved to shake her hand. "Would you like us to give you a quick tour?" Mrs. Puja asked.

"That would be lovely," Ms. Avery said. Mr. Puja gave his wife a somewhat confused look, but went along with the tour anyway. This left Fatima and Marcus alone for a few minutes to say their goodbyes.

"Thanks for a wonderful evening," he said, taking her hand.

"No, thank you for coming," she replied. "I'm sorry about my dad. He really is a good man when you get to know him."

"It's cool," Marcus said with a shrug. "He wasn't so bad."

"Besides, I think he likes you."

"That would be nice."

Fatima giggled. Marcus smiled too, then looked out the door. He could hear the adults moving around the house, so he figured the tour was almost over. Sure enough, the adults were back within the minute.

"Thank you for the tour. This is a very nice home you have here," said Ms. Avery.

"You're quite welcome. You should come again sometime, and we can all have dinner together," Mrs. Puja said.

"I might just have to take you up on that offer."

"Well, you are welcome any time you like."

"Thank you." Ms. Avery smiled, then turned to her son. "I'll wait for you in the car, Marcus. Bye, Fatima." She gave her son's girlfriend a quick hug, then turned and walked out the door. Marcus watched her leave, and once she was in the car, he looked back to Fatima's parents.

"Thanks for dinner," he said, "It was great meeting you."

"Likewise," Mrs. Puja said.

Marcus looked at Fatima. "So, I guess I'll see you in a month then. Try not to miss me too much."

"Too late, Mister," Fatima replied, then wrapped her arms around Marcus and gave him a quick kiss. He smiled and hugged her back, then said another quick "thank you" to her parents before following his mother to the family car.

The big day had finally arrived. Early that morning, Professor Waters arrived with Peter to pick the kids up. They all tossed their gear into the back of the truck, then hopped in and drove off into the unknown.

It took them quite a while to get to their destination, but once they were at the starting point, they picked up their gear and parked the truck in a spot reserved for long-term campers.

"So, I guess this is it," Professor Waters said, looking at Peter.

"Yup. The map starts here, so now we have to head north," he replied. Olivia took a deep breath, then called everyone over.

"I want to say a quick prayer," she said. She bowed her head, and the others did the same. "Dear Lord," she began, "Please protect me and my friends from harm during this journey and let us make it there and back safely. In Jesus' name, Amen."

"Amen."

As they began their trek into the woods, Peter was overcome with a sudden strange feeling. It was a sense of evil, and it prompted him to turn around and look behind. But no matter how hard he looked, he couldn't see anything.

"Hey, are you all right?" Professor Waters asked.

"Ah, yes, I just thought I heard something. Let's keep going," said Peter. The three kids looked at each other in confusion, but kept moving on nonetheless. Not too far from them, however, a raven was perched on a branch, watching them move away. When they had disappeared into the distance, the raven jumped off the branch and flew back down toward the ground, but before it landed, it changed shape. Instead of the bird, there now stood a thin young man with straight black hair and a handful of facial piercings. He was dressed from head to toe in black in a black leather jacket, tight black pants, and matching black military-style boots. He pulled a cell phone out of his pocket and dialed it.

"Justin," the man said, "They've started. Should I pursue?"

"No. We'll give them a head start. Come back to join me and the others; you've done well." The other end of the phone line cut out then, and the man gazed in the direction of Peter and the others, eyes narrowed menacingly. He changed back into a raven and flew away, off to meet his leader.

Nightfall was now upon Peter and the others, and they had quickly found a spot in which to camp out for the night. Peter had gone to gather some wood for a fire, as the night was cold. With the fire going and stomachs content, the conversation started flowing almost immediately.

"So Peter, are you an actual shaman?" Olivia asked. "Like, do you have powers and all that stuff?"

"No, not yet," he replied. "But I've been studying for a while. I don't have any magic powers, but I do have a bit of a sixth sense. I can sense negative forces and energies."

Marcus laughed. "I thought you were gonna say you could see dead people," he joked.

Amused, Peter replied, "No."

"Peter," Professor Waters interrupted, "What made you decide to come on this journey with us?"

"By going on this quest with you, it'll help me to gain knowledge about my people. And who doesn't like a good adventure anyway, right?"

"So do you figure they'll be coming after us?" Tim asked.

"Yes, so we'll have to stay alert. We should all take turns

doing a watch. I can start it off tonight," Peter said. He gestured to a large hunting knife he had brought with him.

Tim raised his eyebrows. "I see you brought a pretty big friend with you."

Peter chuckled. "Yeah, I guess."

"Now," Professor Waters said, standing up and clapping his hands together, "I suggest we make it an early night, so we can get up early tomorrow." Everyone quickly agreed and headed off into the tent, leaving only Peter awake to stand watch.

The next morning, standing at the same point where Tim and the others started, were Justin and ten others. Standing behind him was Orenda, the woman from the fog, as well as Damion, the man who had changed into the shape of a cougar, and John Raven, the punk rocker-looking young man with the facial piercings, who previously been changed into a raven.

Justin turned to look at his followers. "We will walk out of these woods as gods!" he announced. "Once I have the staff, this world will drop to its knees. My friends, we will take back what was stolen from us so many years ago: our history and our heritage. We will make them pay!" He had the full attention of every single person that had come along with him. They were all fired up from his speech. "Are you with me?"

"Yes, we are with you!"

"Okay, then what are we waiting for? Let's go get our prize."

Buzzing with feverish excitement, everyone cheered and began to make their way into the forest in hot pursuit of their target.

CHAPTER 10
The Sweet Song of Farrah

It had been four days since they entered the deep forest when Professor Waters and the rest of the group stumbled into what appeared to be a small oasis. There were lovely fragrant flowers everywhere, and river running through it. It was a scene none of them would have imagined would be there.

Olivia was the first to speak, eyes wide with excitement. "Man, this is beautiful," she said.

"Yes, it is," Professor Waters said, following behind her. "But how could it be in a place like this?"

"I don't know, but let's camp out here for the night," Peter said.

"Cool," said Olivia.

With all the euphoria, they had no idea that they were being watched, and that the danger facing them now was as great as the one that had been chasing them, if not even greater.

As they approached the spot where they were going to camp, Peter noticed that there had been others camping out in the area too, judging by the previous campfire spots on the ground. "Looks like we're not the only ones who have been here," he said. "A few people must have camped out here before, too. Look over there." He pointed to the spots in question, then the professor said, "Yes, you would be correct."

Tim found another spot under a huge oak tree and said, "Hey, this is a great spot to set up camp." Everyone agreed, and they quickly prepared their tents.

Once they had finished, Olivia and Marcus went to pick raspberries from some nearby bushes while the others went fishing in the lake. After they had collected enough food, everyone went for a swim except for the professor, who was gathering firewood when he suddenly heard someone talking to him. He looked around for the source of the voice, but saw nothing, and soon the words turned to song:

"Follow me, I wish to love you... Come with me, I'll be the shelter you need..."

"Professor! Professor, are you okay?"

Professor Waters snapped out of his strange trance and opened his eyes to see Olivia standing right in front of him, a worried look on her face. "Are you all right, Professor?" she repeated.

"Oh, yes, sorry; I was deep in thought," he replied. "By the way, you didn't happen to hear any singing, did you?"

"No sir, I can't say that I have," Olivia responded. "But I'll be singing tonight with my guitar."

"Well, I look forward to that," Professor Waters said.

Olivia smiled and walked away. As she did so, the professor looked around again to see where the voice was coming from, but could no longer hear the song. He gave his head a shake and continued gathering wood for the campfire for the night's food.

With the camp set up and the fire roaring before everyone, night began to fall. As they sat around the fire enjoying the fish they had caught earlier along with some of the food they had brought with them, everyone began to talk about their lives and futures. Eventually, Olivia asked about Shamanism, to which Peter explained to the best of his abilities: "It's more or less about becoming one with nature and your surroundings, and learning about natural ways to live with plants. Magic comes after all of that," he said. "It's used for mostly good, but over the years, some people have tapped into the darker side of the practice, like Justin Sigo. I felt something really evil and powerful within him. We can never let him get his hands on the staff; he would surely use it for corrupt purposes and destruction."

"Well, as long as we stay one step ahead of them, we should be okay to reach our drop-off destination," said Professor Waters.

"Yes, let's hope we can, but we need to keep our eyes open and be suspicious of everything around us, because when you're dealing with magic and shape-shifters, it's hard to know what's real and what isn't," Peter said.

"Do Natives have many legends like this one?" asked Marcus.

"In my culture, there are many story-tellers," Peter answered. "Many stories are passed from generation to generation. It's hard to know what's true and what's not."

"Have you heard stories about these artefacts we have?" Tim asked.

"No, but I've been reading the story since we started this journey."

"Well, I hope where we're taking this stuff is real and not made up, or we're screwed," said Marcus.

"How are we screwed when Tim has so much power?" Olivia asked.

"Hey, I don't know how to make this thing work," Tim responded. "And plus, I don't want it. I just want to get it back where it belongs so I can go back to living a normal life."

"And on that note," Marcus said, "Olivia, won't you pull out that guitar and change the mood a little bit?"

Olivia did as he suggested and whipped out the guitar. She began to strum away at it, singing along to the song that she wrote. Once that one was finished, she moved on to a tune they all wrote together, where Tim and Marcus joined in to sing with her.

"Morning I wake, Sunlight hits my face. I'm realizing things I didn't know yesterday..."

"Wow," Professor Waters said. "You three are even more talented than I thought."

"Thanks," Olivia said, smirking at him before moving on to her final number, a song she'd been working on recently called "Ready For Love" by India Arie, which ended up bringing a bit of somberness to the evening—especially for Tim and Marcus, who were both missing their girlfriends.

From afar, a dangerous presence was watching the group and waiting for the right time to make its presence known.

After the last song, everyone grew tired and decided that it would be best to turn in for the night. Peter offered to stay up and stand watch for the first few hours, and the professor would do the rest. He took some powder from a little pouch he was carrying and poured it in a circle around the camp.

"What's that for?" Olivia asked.

"It's to keep evil out of the camp," he replied. Then, under his breath, he began chanting, *"Cumu lama, cumu lama, cumu lama..."* When he finished, he said, "We're all good."

"All right," Tim said. "We'll see you in the morning, then."

"Good night."

Soon, everyone but Peter had fallen asleep. He was reading more about the story of the staff, but ended up passing out at one point. Once he, too, was asleep, the presence in the woods descended upon the camp, but stopped short of the barrier protecting them. Knowing it couldn't go any further, it vanished into the night.

It was cold the next morning. Over the night, the fire had gone out. Professor Waters had fallen asleep sometime after replacing Peter on guard duty, but luckily was the first to wake up. Feeling a bit chilly and noticing the fire was out, he decided to go out and gather some more wood while everyone was still asleep.

He grabbed his miniature machete and made his way into the woods, but about ten minutes into his search, he began to hear singing. It was the same beautiful singing he had heard the day before. The professor began to move in the direction it was coming from, not stopping until he reached a small clearing. As he approached it, he could see a meadow a lot of flowers. Right in the middle of it stood a stunning young woman.

The woman looked to be about 21 years old. She had dark olive skin and long, shimmering black hair that reached her waistline. Her body was like that of a goddess, with eyes to match. They were the deepest blue the professor had ever seen, and he found himself in awe of her dazzling beauty.

At first, she seemed to ignore the fact that he was watching her as he slowly walked toward the meadow, but at one point, she stopped singing and picked up a flower. She brought it up to her nose to sniff it, closing her eyes and inhaling deeply. When her eyes opened, the woman was looking directly at the professor, and for a moment, it seemed as if her eyes were staring into his very soul.

"Do you like watching me?" she asked.

A little bit embarrassed, Professor Waters got a bit tongue-tied, but eventually managed to stutter out, "Y-yes. Um, I mean, sorry for being so intrusive. I heard your beautiful singing and had to know who you were."

She waved him closer. With every step he took, she seemed more beautiful. "What's your name?" she asked him.

"Mitch Waters," he replied.

"Why are you here?"

"I'm on a quest with my friends."

"A quest?" the woman repeated. "A quest for what?"

"I can't say, but it's very important that we get to our destination."

"Is it now?"

"What's your name?" blurted Professor Waters.

With a small laugh, the woman replied, "Farrah."

"Your name is as beautiful as you are."

"Thank you," replied Farrah, smiling that gorgeous smile of hers.

"Why are you here?" Professor Waters asked.

"This is my home," she responded.

"Really?" The professor raised his eyebrows. "Then where do you live?"

"Close by," she answered. "Come with me; I'll take you there." She stepped forward to take his hand, then slowly began to lead him away. He quietly agreed and followed her, almost in a trance. At this point, he had totally forgotten about the others back at camp. Her spell had been cast, and he was unable to resist her.

Forty minutes after the professor had left them, everyone back at camp had begun to wake up. Marcus was up and stretching, and while he moved, he said, "Man, I had this wild dream. I could hear this singing, and it was beautiful."

"That's funny," Tim said, "Because I had a dream like that, too. It was a woman's voice."

"I had the same dream, too," Peter said.

Olivia frowned. "I didn't; I slept like a baby."

"How can the three of us have had the same dream?" Peter wondered aloud. "There must be some magic invoked here, somehow."

Everyone mumbled amongst themselves until a few minutes later when Olivia asked, "Hey, where's the professor?"

"No idea," Tim said.

Peter shrugged. "I haven't seen him since he took over the guard last night."

"Maybe he went to take a leak?" Marcus suggested.

"Or to get firewood," Tim added.

The three kids started calling out for Professor Waters while Peter hung back and tried to figure out how they all had the same dream. He began to meditate, but soon began to sense both positive and negative energies around the camp. Thinking about the various energies floating about, he began to reflect on his past, to moments when he was a kid and his grandfather would tell stories to him and the other kids. One in particular stood out at the moment: the story of the witch named Farrah, who lived in the woods.

The story told of a witch who would sing a beautiful song to lure men to her and take their lives. She was said to be beautiful on the outside, but disgustingly ugly on the inside, filled with pure evil. The tale had scared Peter as a child.

Suddenly, he snapped out of his trance with a loud gasp. Everyone looked at him, worried for their friend. "What's wrong?" Tim asked.

"Farrah."

"Who's Farrah?" Olivia asked.

"A very dangerous witch," Peter replied. "The professor might be in danger. Let's go."

Everyone quickly grabbed up the artefacts and headed

into the woods, following behind the shaman, who was leading the way. He was quick to track the professor, eventually coming upon a pile of twigs that may have been used for firewood.

"He must have stopped here," Peter said. He looked down at the pile of twigs again and pointed it out to the kids. "This is where she probably got him."

"Hold up, man," Marcus said. "Who is this witch Farrah and how do you know she has him? Or if she's even real?"

"There's no other explanation," Peter answered. "When I was a kid, my grandfather told us a story of a cursed witch who lives in this forest. She's supposedly very beautiful and sings to lure men to her, then kills them. All three of us could hear the song, but not Olivia. I think Professor Waters must have heard her too and gone to investigate, and that's why he's probably missing now."

"Well, let's hope we find him before it's too late," Tim said.

They all began to follow the trail again, through the meadow and back into the woods until they came across an old cottage.

"I bet she's in there with him," Tim said.

"Yeah. It's a cute place, but kinda creepy," Olivia agreed.

"We don't have any time to waste," Peter said. "We'll have to rush the cabin and hope he's still alive."

"On the count of three, then," Olivia said. "One... two... three!"

On the count of three, the four of them took off at a run for the cottage.

Inside, Farrah could sense their presence; however, it wasn't their presence that worried her, but that of something very powerful that they had with them. For a second, she lost her focus, and her true self was revealed: her dark hair had turned grey and wiry while her skin dried up and sagged from her face. Her lips were left thin, dry, and cracked, nothing like the full, soft lips they had been a moment ago. Farrah's eyes were still blue, but their vibrancy had dulled and they had sunken back into their sockets. She laughed a dry, wheezing chuckle, snorting quietly as she lay on the bed.

Professor Waters was shocked. He was hovering above Farrah, shirt off. When she realized what had happened, the witch tried to grab his head to pull him back down into a kiss so she could continue to drain his life away, but he jerked back before she could get a good grip on him.

Falling back to the floor and breathing heavily with fear, he shouted, "What are you?!"

"A woman," she replied coldly. "Don't you like me? Or did you like me better when I was beautiful?"

Farrah immediately dropped the presence. Now she was her true self. She got off the bed and began to advance on the man before her. Still on the floor, Professor Waters started moving backward on his hands until he bumped into something. It fell from its perch, landing right between his legs. When he looked down at it, the professor realized it was a human skull.

"Oh, shit!" he screamed, then looked around the house to see other dried-up corpses lying around. He got up and ran for the door, but couldn't open it. Outside, the others could hear him and tried to break the door down, but couldn't seem to do it.

Farrah walked slowly toward the professor, whose back was now against the door. "Get away from me!" he yelled.

"You can't get out," she replied. "And they can't get in. Besides, I can't let you leave without a goodbye kiss."

She began chanting, and all of a sudden Professor Waters felt his body freeze in place.

"I can't move!" he shouted. "Oh, God!"

Farrah smiled and got up on him, face-to-face. "You are very handsome," she said. "There's something about you I like. You wouldn't have lasted this long otherwise."

Outside, the others were trying desperately to knock the door down, but to no avail. Tim was getting so frustrated with this that he hit the door with the staff, and somehow it broke the door open, knocking both the professor and the witch to the floor.

"How'd you do that?" Olivia asked.

"I don't know," answered Tim. He looked around the room, trying to find where he'd knocked the professor, and noticed Farrah attempting to stand. For a second, she levitated, hovering up above the ground and poised to attack, but after taking a look at the staff, she moved away to cower in the corner of the room.

Olivia looked around "Eww, this is sick," she said. Then she saw the professor half-dressed and wrinkled her nose at him. "Man, put some clothes on!"

"Damn!" Marcus adding, moving to stand next to Olivia and nudge her arm. "The professor was about to get his freak on!" He let out a chuckle and Olivia rolled her eyes.

"Men."

"Please don't hurt me!" Farrah said.

"Hurt you?" repeated Peter. "Look at what you did to these men!"

"They came here to hurt my animals," Farrah responded. "They deserved what they got." Her eyes darted to the staff. "How did you get the Staff of the Four Winds?"

"You know of this staff?" the shaman asked.

"Yes, I've seen its great power."

"What do you mean?" asked the professor. "What have you seen?"

"I've seen many die at the hand of the staff," she said, then began to tell the story of the Great War back in the 1800's, where the staff wiped out thousands of people. The greed of a single shaman had been what caused it.

By the time she had finished, Farrah had returned to her beautiful form. Once again, she asked, "How did you get that staff?"

"I found it in a cave in the woods," Tim replied.

"How can this be? My father took it to a holy place."

"If you mean the Island of the Ancients," said Professor Waters, "He never made it. I believe he died in a cave with it, along with three other shamans."

All of a sudden Farrah began to tear up. She raised her hands to her face and began to sob. In pain, she screamed, "No! Not my papa!" With another great, heaving sob she fell to her knees. "That's why he didn't come for me when they took me."

"I'm sorry for your loss," said Peter. "But who took you, and how did you get here?"

Farrah took a moment to calm herself. When she was more relaxed, she explained that right after the Great War and after her father left on his journey with the staff, she was taken in the middle of the night by three evil shamans that wanted to get even with her father. They cursed her to roam the woods, never to leave again, and used a spell to take away her beauty. One of the shamans had been in love with her, and with the others not knowing, had left her a book of spells and magic.

"From that, I learned how to cast spells and keep my beauty by taking the essence from others that would harm me or the animals," she said. "But I'm not evil like legend would have you believe."

"She is right," Peter said. "That's why I didn't sense her."

Farrah looked at Tim. "You are white man. Why don't you use the staff for evil?"

"Because times have changed," Tim said, "and I want to finish what your father started. I want to get the staff to the Island of the Ancients."

Farrah paused, looked at Tim for a few more moments, then said, "I sense that you're a good man."

"There are evil people after us," Peter said. "One is a shaman that is very powerful. They want the staff, so we have to get it to the Island before they get to us."

"There's a shortcut to get there," Farrah said. She pointed out the way for them to go. "There are people who live by the water that protect the island. They can help you against the evil ones if they can get past me. I'll try to hold off as many as I can."

"Thank you."

Everyone agreed to leave right away. They went back to their camp and packed up, continuing their journey as Farrah looked on.

CHAPTER 11
The Journey Continues

The further everyone walked away, the more of a blur Farrah became.

"Man," Marcus said, "All this stuff is crazy. Witches, magic, it's like I'm living in a dream."

"What do you think will happen to her?" Olivia asked.

"I don't know," replied Professor Waters.

"I really feel sorry for her."

"Why y'all feel so sorry for her?" Marcus asked. "She probably killed tons of people."

"You have to remember that she's very old and her soul has been tortured for all these years," said Peter. "She still thinks the white man is out to hurt our people. That's all she knows."

"I guess I didn't look at it that way. I feel you," said Marcus.

"Well, all I know for certain is that we've got to see this thing through. I've seen what she spoke of in my dreams and what I saw was pretty scary," Tim said.

"That's why we're all here," replied Peter. "We will see this journey through together."

Later that evening, they found a place to settle down and make camp. By the time they got the fire going and the tents up, it was already nightfall.

It was a full moon, and the night sounds were out full-force. The stars were out by the thousands. It was a perfect night to sit in front of the fire. Tonight, the mood was more somber than it had previously been. The events that had played out early that morning were still fresh in everyone's mind, as was the journey ahead. The importance of their task had really hit home.

"I can't wait to get home and eat some of my mom's good cooking," Olivia said.

"Girl, you're preaching to the choir," Marcus replied. Everyone laughed.

"So, Tim, what are your dreams like?" Peter asked.

"Usually I see a boy with this staff. He has tears in his eyes and he's looking over what seems to be a bunch of bodies and total destruction," Tim explained. 'Then he'll look at me and he'll say things like he's warning me about something. Then sometimes I'll see Justin talking to me, yelling at me, watching me and it scares me sometimes."

"I don't think these are just dreams. Justin might be getting into your head by using black magic," Peter said. "And when the time is right, we'll stop him."

After a while, everyone started to get tired, so they decided to go to sleep. They all went into their own tents, except Peter, who stayed up to meditate. It wasn't long after everyone fell asleep that he noticed a raven in the tree, watching over them. Something about it didn't sit well with the shaman, so he got up to investigate. Before he could reach the bird, however, he heard Tim murmuring in his sleep. Deciding that was more important, Peter turned around and went to check on Tim.

When he reached Tim's tent, it was obvious that the teenager was in distress. He was yelling in his sleep, calling for someone to get out of his head. Peter, thinking he might have been talking about Justin, ran to get his bag and pulled out a dream catcher. He brought it back to Tim's tent, but the ruckus managed to wake the others up as well, and they quickly joined him to see what was going on.

Peter placed the dream catcher above Tim's head and started chanting, and Tim began to shake uncontrollably.

"Justin!" Peter yelled out. "You have no business here! You are not welcome! Leave him!"

He continued to chant, and then all of a sudden Justin Sigo's face appeared in the net of the dream catcher. "You cannot stop me!" it screamed. "I will get the staff and you will all pay with your lives!"

With one last cry, the face disappeared and Peter fell to the ground, out of breath from the strain of the spell. He took a couple of deep breaths, then yelled out, "The raven!" and jumped up to run outside. When he was out of the tent, Peter grabbed a rock and threw it at the raven. It flew off just before it was hit, departing with a loud shriek.

Everyone looked at Peter with a mixture of confusion and worry, as if he had lost his mind. He turned to see their bewildered faces and said, "What? I could sense evil in that bird. I thought it might have been a spy for Justin."

When they didn't respond, Peter sighed. "You don't understand, do you? They know where we are."

"What was the deal with Tim?" Marcus blurted. "Was he possessed or what?"

"No," Peter replied, "But he was being attacked through his dreams. I used the dream catcher to pull him out and block Justin from invading his mind again."

"Wow, they really work," Olivia said.

"Yes, when you know how to use it."

There was a sound overhead, like flapping wings. Peter looked up and saw the raven again, and acting unassumingly, quickly grabbed a rock and threw it. This time, he managed to nip the bird's wing before it flew off.

"Tell Justin we will never give him the staff without a fight!" he called after it. "Do you hear me, Justin?"

Then, out of nowhere, a flock of ravens flew at the group, knocking Peter to the ground. Everyone else ducked, but as soon as they had come, they had flown off again into the night.

"I think he got the message loud and clear," Professor Waters said.

Lying on the ground, Marcus replied, "This shit is off the chain, for real."

Meanwhile, not very far away, Justin Sigo was meditating before a campfire. He was focusing on a spell that enabled him to see through Raven's eyes. When he opened his eyes, Justin looked up to see a flock of ravens: the same one that had attacked his rivals before. He patiently looked on as they flew toward him. When they were just in front of Justin, the ravens converged to form a thin young man, who looked around 28 years old, with a punk rocker/emo appearance. He wore a black leather jacket with ripped t-shirt under it, tight dark jeans, and military-style boots. He had long straight black hair, piercings (two rings particularly in his lip and in his nose), dark makeup around his eyes, and dark lipstick. Around his neck, he wore a leather necklace with a black claw hanging from it.

"Good job, Raven," he said. Then, noticing a small wound, asked, "What happened to your arm?"

"They got wise to me and one of them threw a rock, but I'll be okay," Raven replied. "Did you get to see enough?"

"I did, and I believe we're in stalking distance. Oh, and don't worry, they found me out too, but no matter." Justin sneered. "The end of this cat and mouse game is close, and once I get the staff, nothing and nobody will be able to stop me. I'll be invincible."

Back at the other camp, everyone had calmed down a bit after the recent drama. Peter again said he would stand watch, and once again, everyone headed into their tents, albeit more jittery than before. Olivia grabbed the rosary she had brought in with her and prayed until she fell asleep.

In her sleep, Olivia tossed and turned. Eventually she sat up and, still asleep and wrapped in the wolf's hide, she began to walk on all fours. Soon her body morphed into that of a wolf's, and she left her tent.

Seeing her like this startled Peter at first, as he did not recognize Olivia. Soon, however, he sensed that there was no danger, and simply watched as the wolf made its way to the forest, where it let out a wail. The cry was different than anything the shaman had ever heard before, and he listened with rapt attention as the song died out. Then, as suddenly as it had stopped, what sounded like hundreds of wolves burst out in response.

Rustling was coming from the forest; it awoke the others. They stood outside their tents in amazement as the rustling trees and bushes revealed hundreds of eyes in the darkness surrounding the camp's perimeter. The white wolf then turned back to look at the others, who watched with jaws gone slack in awe of the scene before them. Ignoring them, the white wolf made its way back into Olivia's tent.

After a minute of staring, the others followed it to find Olivia fast asleep with the wolf's hide still wrapped around her. Once again, everyone looked at each other and slowly backed out of the tent.

"She called the wolves to protect us tonight. We are safe," Peter said.

"Safe?" replied Marcus. "How can you say we're safe with a pack of wolves surrounding us?"

"It's okay. We can sleep, all of us."

Marcus threw his hands up as he walked back to his tent, mumbling, "I must be going crazy."

Everyone else went back to their respective tents as well, much too tired to try and wrap their heads around what had happened this time.

When everyone had woken up the next morning, the wolves were gone. Everyone but Olivia gave each other questioning looks, wondering if what they had seen last night was real. Olivia was the last to wake; when she got up, she said, "Man, I had this crazy dream last night."

Marcus was quick to jump in. "Let me guess. You were a wolf and you was kicking it with other wolves?"

"Something like that," Olivia replied. "How did you know?"

"You can call it a good guess."

Olivia looked confused by this answer, and was even more surprised when the others chuckled a bit. Professor Waters was quick to interrupt this. "Let's pack 'em up. We've got a long day ahead of us," he said.

Once they had cleaned up their camp, they continued on their journey deep into the woods. Still baffled, Olivia asked, "Why were y'all laughing?"

Marcus smiled and put his arm around her shoulder. "No reason, sis. Let's go."

Meanwhile, a few miles away, Justin and his companions were already hot on their trail. The group of 20 reached the same spot their rivals had been, by the lake surrounded by beauty. Like the others before, the group was in awe of the scene in the middle of the forest.

One of the men of the group, the main tracker, soon caught sight of the dead campfires and pointed them out to Justin. "They left this place a few days ago, but they were here," he said.

Justin nodded and looked around. "This place is not natural," he said. "This is magic."

All of a sudden they could hear something in the woods. "There's somebody out there," Justin said. "Let's split up and see who's hiding."

Once they had split up, the same enchanting song that had lulled Professor Waters began again. It drew each person to a different area. Then, like a ghost, Farrah began to appear in front of them. Her beauty mesmerized, intoxicated, and enchanted them all at once. Like others that had crossed the path before, the men were powerless to resist.

"Why have you come here?" Farrah asked the first one.

"We're looking for some others," he answered quietly, in a daze.

"Would there be some young ones with them?" she asked.

"Yes."

With a coy grin, she walked up to the man. "Kiss me," she said. He leaned in without hesitation. Within a minute of their kiss, the man's body began to shake. His skin turned grey and dried up until it was nothing more than a corpse. She pushed it away from her and it fell to the ground, where she watched it for a second as it lay lifeless. But she heard another man approaching her, which drew her attention away. As soon as he was upon her, she smiled and repeated the same process, until five corpses lay at her feet.

The sixth man to face her was a man dressed in all black. Farrah could sense that there was something special about him. She could tell that he was the leader of the group, and killing him might help the young ones get to the island and fulfill their quest.

She approached him with caution and asked, "Are you their leader?"

"Yes, I am the leader of this group, Justin Sigo," the man said. "And who might you be?"

"I am Farrah."

Justin paused to think for a minute, then replied, "Oh,

Farrah. So the legend is true. You are as beautiful as they say. Not at all the grotesque creature I've read about. Might I assume many men had to die for you to maintain such youth and beauty?"

"Maybe," replied Farrah. "You are quite handsome yourself," she answered.

"Thank you. I must apologize for my ancestor, who was one of those who banished you here to this place."

Hearing this made Farrah angry, but she managed to hold her rage inside, knowing that he would soon be her next victim. "That was long ago," she said. "And this is now. And right now, you're all I want."

Speechless, Justin stood there, almost in a daze as he watched her gown fall to her feet. Farrah was naked now, displaying every inch of her goddess-like beauty. Slowly, she began to walk toward him. His eyes welcomed her approach and his heart beat rapidly. He knew how deadly she was, yet he couldn't seem to resist. Every inch of him ached for her touch.

Once she was in front of him, Justin reached out to touch Farrah's face. She responded by nuzzling into his palm. The action made Justin's heart melt, and desire rose in him like it had never risen before.

"Take me, Justin," she whispered to him, voice low and sultry. "Take me now."

So great was his desire that Justin took the witch in his arms and began to kiss her passionately, and so intensely that he didn't realize she was drawing the life force from his body until it was too late. The process had begun, and now he couldn't break free. His eyes opened first, wide with terror, then hers were revealed as well, black and soulless. As hard as he tried, he couldn't break free, nor could he speak up in protest.

As Justin was just about to face his doom, there was a light tap on Farrah's shoulder. She quickly turned around, and standing in front of her was Orenda. Justin fell to the ground, forgotten, as Orenda lunged forward and began to kiss Farrah.

Smoke began billowing from Farrah's mouth, eyes, and ears. Her beautiful image faded until she was left in her true form as the toxic smoke Orenda forced into the witch's body began to slowly poison her. When they broke apart, Farrah took one last look at her murderer and whispered, "I'm free."

She fell backward to the ground, changing into her beautiful form for the last time before she died.

Orenda looked at Justin and sneered. "Men," she said. "They just can't keep it in their pants." She looked down at Farrah sadly.

"So beautiful. What a waste." Then, looking back over to Justin, Orenda barked, "Come on, Lover boy!" and walked off.

Justin stood, but could barely keep his balance. He struggled to get his bearings for a few minutes, but eventually moved on with the rest of his crew to continue their pursuit.

CHAPTER 12
The People by the Water

L ater that night, Professor Waters and the others found a nice spot and set up camp. It was a bit colder than the last few nights, so they all sat close to the fire to warm their hands and feet. As they were talking, Tim said, "I wish we hadn't found this stuff, then we wouldn't be in this situation."

"I think the staff chose you, Tim," Peter replied.

"Why?" Tim asked. "I just don't get it. I'm white, and my ancestors treated your people terribly. Why would it have chosen me of all people?"

"I don't know why, but I'm sure there's a grand purpose in all of this."

"Man, I don't know about none of this stuff," Marcus jumped in. "We just need to get it done so I can go back to a normal life."

"Hear hear," Olivia said.

"I believe we are all here for a reason," said Professor Waters, "And no matter what we are all in this together." He extended his hand, and one by one, everyone put their hands on top of his as a show of unity.

The next morning was a beautiful one. Tim and the others got up bright and early to continue their journey. They walked for hours until they came to another clearing in the woods. This one was not as nice as the one where they had met Farrah, but they explored it just the same, and ended up coming across some fruit trees. There were apple, cherry, peach, and pear trees, as well as a large garden. Excited, Olivia shouted out, "Hey, look everyone! An apple tree!"

"Wow, it sure is," Professor Waters replied.

"Someone must have planted the trees and garden here. You would never find these types of fruit in the middle of the forest," Peter observed. "Be on guard. I don't believe we are alone."

"Okay," Marcus said, "But in the meantime, I'm fixin' to grab a bunch of these."

"Me too!" Olivia exclaimed.

They all proceeded to stock up on fruit, picking the apples from the trees, as well as gathering raspberries and plucking pears from other branches. Once they were loaded up, they continued on their quest. It wasn't long before Peter began feeling uneasy, however. He felt as if something wasn't right, and sensed danger ahead. "Keep your eyes open; I feel like we're being watched," he said.

"Word. Something does seem strange," Marcus replied.

"A little paranoid, are we fellas?" Olivia asked. She laughed and lifted one of the apples to her lips, ready to sink her teeth into it. Right before she could, however, an arrow soared toward her and knocking it out of her hand and pinning it to a nearby tree.

"What the *hell*?" Olivia shouted. In the blink of an eye, out of the forest came what appeared to be about thirty Native warriors, carrying old weapons: tomahawks, spears, bows and arrows. They surrounded the group of travelers, one of them asking in his tongue, "Why are you here? Why do you trespass on this land?"

The kids turned to Peter, not understanding what had been said to them. The shaman, however, understood perfectly, and responded in the same language, "We are very sorry for intruding on your land. We are on a quest to find the Island of the Ancients and we were told the People by the Water could help us find the place. Do you know of such a people?"

Stunned, the warrior that had spoken before asked, "How did you hear of such a tribe?"

"From the witch, Farrah."

The warriors all glanced back and forth between each other, surprised. "Why do you seek the Island of the Ancients?"

"We need its protection."

"Can he help us?" Olivia asked. Peter quickly asked the same question.

The warrior looked at his companions, then back at the

group they had surrounded, and nodded his head. "Come," he said, turning to Peter. He began to walk away, and the others followed without hesitation.

"Hey," Marcus whispered. "What if they're all cannibals and they think all black people taste like chicken?"

Olivia laughed quietly and joined in, saying, "Yeah, and all Mexican people probably taste like fajitas!" They both let out a small chuckle, and Tim whipped his head around to glare at them.

"Will you two cut it out? We have to take this seriously," he hissed.

"Okay, okay," Marcus said. He stayed quiet for a few minutes, then under his breath, he said to Olivia, "I wonder what they think white people taste like."

"Probably like Wonder Bread," Olivia responded.

"Yeah. In the hood, chicken tastes good on Wonder Bread, so I wonder if it's the same in their hood?" Marcus replied, grinning broadly. The two began to snicker again, holding their hands over their mouths to contain an all-out laugh assault. All Tim could do was roll his eyes and shake his head.

After 45 minutes of traveling, they came to a village by a massive lake. It consisted of several old-style wood cabins, and there was a faint scent of musk and smoke in the air. Before they could enter the village, the head warrior asked them to wait where they were. He took some of his men with him and entered the village while the remaining warriors stood guard. While they were gone, Marcus whispered, "Hey y'all, is it just me or do y'all smell something funky, too?"

"Get used to it, Marcus," Peter said. "These villagers probably don't wear deodorant and cologne like you and I."

"Eww, that's nasty," Olivia said. Peter and Professor Waters laughed at her comment, and Peter prepared to explain the cultural significance behind this, but before he could get a word out, the professor put his hand on the shaman's shoulder.

"My young friend, leave well enough alone. Don't try to explain; they won't get it," he said. Peter gave him a quick nod in agreement.

The next ten minutes were spent in quiet but nervous anticipation, until the first warriors returned.

"Follow me," their leader said. Peter stepped after him, and the others followed behind them. He led them on a dirt path through the village, passing by the small cabins. As they passed, the newcomers drew states from the villagers who were out and about. Most of the people watching were wearing traditional Native clothes, like they were still living in the past. This intrigued Peter more than anything else.

Finally, they came to a house set aside from the others. The warrior leading them knocked on the door, and a beautiful young woman dressed in traditional Native garb answered. She was tall and had long black hair that went just past her breast. Her lips were full, and she had bright hazel eyes. She and the lead warrior conversed in their language for a minute, and then the woman turned to the outsiders and greeted them in English. "Welcome."

The men in the group were awestruck as they followed behind her into the house. "Damn, she's fine," Marcus whispered to Tim.

"Who you telling?" Tim replied.

Olivia rolled her eyes. "You guys are pigs," she hissed. Professor Waters let out a quiet chuckle. Peter, on the other hand, seemed completely oblivious to the conversation around him. He, too, was mesmerized by the woman's beauty, but remained silent.

When they made it to the main room, they found a man sitting in a rocking chair by the fireplace and smoking a pipe. He looked to be about sixty and wore his hair in two braids that went just past his shoulders. He was wearing traditional clothing as well, but he also had a black knitted blanket draped over his shoulders.

"This is my father," the woman said in her native tongue, "And the chief of this tribe."

Though only Peter could understand her dialect, everyone else seemed to understand that the man was in charge.

He looked at his daughter and the warrior accompanying the group, dismissing them quietly in his language. Then, in English, he addressed the group of travelers. "Welcome. I am Chief Masaka of Nantego. Please have a seat."

Everyone did as they were asked, glancing at each other uneasily. Chief Masaka nodded solemnly. "You have come far," he said. "How did you make it past the witch, Farrah, when so many have died in her presence, and how did you make it here to my people?"

"We almost didn't," Peter replied, "It was only when she learned of our quest that we were able to pass."

"And what might this quest be?" asked Chief Masaka.

"We need to go to the Island of the Ancients to return three artefacts that these kids found in a cave. The witch said you could help us."

Tim gestured toward the staff he held, and Chief Masaka focused his attention on it. "May I take a closer look?" he asked.

"Sure," Tim replied as he handed it over.

Chief Masaka examined it for a minute, then read the words on the talisman out loud in English: "Only the pure of heart—" he gasped suddenly, eyes going wide as the staff fell from his hands. It was almost as if he had seen a ghost.

"Are you all right, Chief?" asked Peter.

"Yes," he replied. "You say you found this in a cave?"

"Yes, sir."

"Do you know what power you possess?"

"Yes sir, I think so. That's why we need to get these artefacts to the Island before Justin and his associates find us."

Chief Masaka frowned, puzzled. "Who is Justin?" he asked.

"An evil shaman that wishes to unleash the power of the staff upon the world," Peter said. "We can't let that happen."

"I understand, and you are correct," said Chief Masaka. "Evil must not possess this staff. We will make our way to the Island of the Ancients first thing in the morning."

Word had spread throughout the village about the newcomers. Chief Masaka had organized a special dinner, dance, and story-telling event in honor of the guests. The tribe had collectively provided lodging and traditional clothing for the ceremony. This excited everyone, but Peter especially.

Just before the ceremony, Peter decided to take a walk by the river. He had already dressed in preparation for the ceremony, so he had time to spare. When he arrived at the water's edge, he was surprised to find the chief's daughter sitting there. He approached her quietly. "Do you mind if I sit here?" he asked.

"No."

"Oh, so you do speak English?"

"Yes, we all do," the woman replied. "But most of us choose to speak in our Native language. We believe in keeping our traditions alive." She sighed and looked down at the water threatening to touch her toes. "I've lived in the big city before, as many of us here have, and I hated it. This is where I belong, with my people."

"I understand," Peter said. "It's beautiful here."

A few moments of silence stretched out, with the shaman fidgeting a little nervously next to the chief's daughter. He took a deep breath, then finally worked up the courage to ask, "Do you have a boyfriend? You're very beautiful."

"Thank you," she replied with a small smile. "And no, I don't. My last boyfriend lived here with us, but wanted more, and left for the city. I went with him. I wanted to come home, but he didn't, so I left him there. I haven't been with anyone since." Her eyes moved up to the shaman. "Do you have anyone?"

"No, I'm single," Peter replied. "My girlfriend and I broke up recently."

"Why?"

"We were on different paths in life, I suppose."

"I understand."

"I like how your tribe has preserved our culture," Peter said after a few more seconds of silence. "I've never seen anything like this before."

"I love my life and my people. That's why I came back." She smiled at him again. "This was my path to take. Do you know what yours is?"

Before he could answer, the faint sound of a distant horn filled the air. The chief's daughter jumped up. "I have to leave now. You need to join your friends for the ceremony."

Just as she was about to run off, Peter hurriedly said, "Wait! What's your name?"

"Mahay," she replied, smiling before she turned and ran off. Peter sat there alone for another few minutes, reflecting on her and everything that had happened to him up until this point. He tossed a couple of rocks in the water before finally standing up and leaving to join his friends.

Peter and the others were special guests tonight, and in honor of their visit and their quest they were being treated to a night of traditional native food, dancing, and storytelling, much to their delight. Mahay was participating in the dance. The dance was unlike anything the kids had ever seen before; they felt like they were watching an old movie. The dancers seemed as if they were in a trance, swept up by the beat of the drums and waving their arms around to it. They jumped around and stomped their feet as they chanted. Although the kids and Professor Waters were enraptured by the dance, throughout the entire event, she and Peter couldn't keep their eyes off each other. This did not go unnoticed by Tim and the others when they finally looked away, nor was it missed by the chief.

After the dance, the tribe's shaman performed a ritual to communicate with the spirit world. He was dressed in what looked like aprons made of animal hide, a bearskin robe, and several handmade necklaces strung with different kinds of animal teeth and charms, many of which also bore symbols. In one hand was a rattle, and in the other he held a skin drum. His headdress resembled a crane's head. To start the ritual, he approached the bonfire in the middle of the group and raised his hands. *"Oh baaa ne nak nak na, ne nak nak na..."* he chanted. The fire steadily grew higher and higher and the shaman walked around it, still chanting and shaking his rattle. Every few steps, he would hit the drum with the rattle. As he moved, different images were formed inside the fire—sometimes faces faded in and out, and sometimes animals appeared and disappeared.

The kids sat there in awe, all their attention focused on the ritual, finding it hard to believe what they were seeing. But in the middle of it, the shaman stopped what he was doing and turned to look at Tim, then gazed at him with a crazed look in his eye. He glanced at Tim, then Chief Masaka, and walked over to the chief to whisper in his ear. Though he looked concerned, the chief nodded his head, and the two men looked back at the group. The ritual and ceremony then ended, and Chief Masaka thanked his guests before they went back to their lodging for the night.

A few hours later, the lead warrior from before approached the group of kids and the professor. "The chief would like to see you at his home," he told them. They obediently hiked to the cabin where they had met Chief Masaka, and found him there with the shaman that had performed the ritual. "Come in," he said.

The group stepped inside and sat down, waiting to find out why they had been summoned. They weren't waiting long: Chief Masaka gestured to the shaman standing next to him and said, "This is our village's shaman, Woodo. Before you go to sleep tonight, we would like to have a word with you."

Woodo quickly approached Tim and began to speak. "You possess great power," he said. "There are some that would kill to have it. I sense you all are in great danger, and we must get you to the Island tomorrow at the first chance."

"We will keep an eye out for others intruding on our land," Chief Masaka added. "For now, get some rest, and prepare for your journey."

"Thank you," said Professor Waters. With that, everyone stood up to leave but Peter, who decided he would stay behind and speak with Woodo. Being a young shaman himself, Peter was very interested in learning from someone more experienced than he was.

"Woodo," Peter began, "I want to learn more about being a shaman. Can you teach me?"

Woodo replied, "Young shaman, there is so much you must learn. My father was a shaman, and his father was a shaman, and so on, going back for centuries. I would like to share my knowledge with you as they did with me, but right now, time is not on your side."

A disappointed look appeared on Peter's face. "I understand. Thank you anyway," he said, then turned to walk away.

Woodo paused for a second, then took a step forward. "Young shaman, come here," he said. Peter turned around, surprised, and did as he was told. "Give me your hands."

Peter reached over and put his palms on top of Woodo's, and the elder shaman closed his eyes and began mumbling under his breath. His face began to start changing expressions and his body twitched and swayed as if he were in the middle of a nightmare. Then, all of a sudden, he stopped and his eyes opened wide, like a deer in headlights.

"You have a sixth sense like me," he whispered. "You can sense negative energy. I could see what you have seen. These people that pursue you... they are shape-shifters, yes?"

"Yes," Peter responded.

"I sense that their leader is a diablero—a powerful dark shaman. He must not get the staff. If he does, we shall all die by his hand." Woodo looked up into Peter's eyes. "My people and I will help you as much as we can."

After they finished speaking, Peter headed to where his friends were staying. Once again, he ran into Mahay, whom he noticed was wearing many necklaces and pendants. "Oh... Hello," he said.

"Hi," she said. There was a moment of awkward silence before Mahay continued," I know you're in danger. I overheard my father speaking with you."

"Yeah, well... What's life without a little danger, right?" Peter returned.

Clearly not amused, she replied, "You and your friends should be careful."

"We will try."

She then reached behind her head and took off one of the necklaces she had been wearing, then carefully draped it over Peter's neck.

"Wow," he breathed. "Thank you."

"It's for good luck," Mahay replied before Peter could ask why she did that.

"But I don't want to take something I'm sure means a lot to you," he responded.

"It does mean a lot to me; it was a gift from my mother for good luck and protection. It's the symbol of the wolf, and I'm lending it to you so you will be safe. You can return it when your quest is finished."

"Agreed."

She laughed quietly and kissed Peter on the cheek before leaving. Peter stared after her for a minute. He was completely smitten. Once he had taken everything in, he looked down at the necklace again and smiled before tucking it into his shirt and continuing on to his cabin.

Inside the cabin, Tim was fast asleep and beginning to dream. First, images of Josette flitted through his dreams, then his friends. After cycling through a few fond memories, Tim once again found himself back in the 1800's, in the midst of the Great War's death and destruction. He could see the same boy standing with tears in his eyes, staring at him. Tim could feel his pain and sadness more acutely than ever before, but the boy then turned around to start walking back to his village in slow motion, stopping only to point behind Tim. Tim turned around to see his friends lying spread-eagle on the ground, eyes closed and bruises spread all over their bodies.

"Are they dead?" he called out to the boy, but he had already vanished. When Tim turned back to look at his friends once more, they had gone too. The next thing he knew, he had woken up in a cold sweat.

He looked around quickly to see if Marcus and the others were all right, and much to his relief, they were sound asleep. Marcus was even snoring loudly. Tim stood up and walked over to the window. The wind began to pick up a little, and for a second, Tim thought he could see the boy from his dreams again, standing out front and gazing in his direction.

Just then a hand fell on Tim's shoulder and startled him. He almost jumped out of his skin, but was quickly calmed when he realized it was only Peter.

"Are you all right?" the shaman asked.

"Shit, man, you surprised me," Tim replied.

"Hey, I'm sorry. I saw you up and thought maybe you couldn't sleep because things were weighing heavy on your mind."

"Nah, I'm okay, I just had another crazy dream."

"Whatever these dreams are trying to tell you, you really have to try and focus and listen to what they're saying," Peter said.

"I think they're warnings."

"Maybe they are, my friend. That's even more reason to find an answer."

"You're right," said Tim. "Next time, I'll try harder."

"Good." Peter clapped Tim's shoulder. "Now let's get some sleep; we have a quest to finish."

"I'm right behind you, man." Tim grinned. "Thanks for the talk."

"Anytime. We're all in this together, after all."

Peter moved to lay back down, leaving Tim to look out the window one last time before laying down and going back to sleep. One his eyes were closed and his mind had shut down, the spirit of the boy from Tim's dreams materialized at the window for a few seconds, watching everyone before disappearing once more.

CHAPTER 13
The Fight for the Staff

The morning had broken and it was time for Tim and the others to continue on with their quest. The end was in sight now; they could all feel it. While they began to pack up their gear, some of the village's warriors stationed themselves at the outskirts of the village where the fruit trees grew. They soon came upon a lone man in a long black trench coat standing there, biting into an apple. He had dark curly hair, dark eyes, and a scruffy five o'clock shadow of a beard. The men quickly surrounded him and asked, "Why are you here?"

"Hey, I'm just minding my own business and enjoying this apple," the man replied.

"You do not belong here on our land," said the head warrior.

"Hey, sorry. I didn't see the sign, my bad."

"You will come with us," the warriors said.

"I don't think so."

All of a sudden, a fog began to cover the ground. The warriors were baffled. "What is this?" one of them asked. The man just smirked deviously.

"Your worst nightmare."

The warriors couldn't move their legs where they were

surrounded by fog. The man in front of them morphed into a flock of ravens, each one flying up and diving toward the Native warriors. By the time the last Raven charged, the entire band of warriors, save one, had fallen to the ground unconscious. Before the last one fell, however, he managed to sound his horn to warn the rest of the village of the impending danger. Just as he was blowing his instrument, the fog slithered up his body and crawled into it, making the warrior choke violently before falling to the ground, dead.

Once the men had all fallen, out of the fog came Justin Sigo and the rest of his crew. The ravens once again joined together to take the form of a man, and the fog solidified into the shape of a woman. Raven and Orenda both took their positions at Justin's side.

"So much for the subtle approach," Justin said. "I can sense they're here, and now I'm sure they know we're here too. Be ready to fight."

"Always," replied Orenda. "Now let's go finish this."

At the village of Nantego, the horn was heard by all. It created panic among the villagers; Peter and Woodo could immediately sense evil in the area. Another horn sounded out, this time from Chief Masaka, signalling that it was time for everyone to retreat and evacuate. It took only a few moments for all the women and children of the village to be gathered up. When they had been collected, they were taken to a remote cave for their protection.

Once they felt that everyone was safe, Chief Masaka and Woodo joined with the tribe's remaining warriors, formulating a plan and eventually splitting up. The leader of the band of warriors, Coakley, took his men to defend the perimeter of the village, while some others were stationed outside the cave to protect the women and children. Chief Masaka, Woodo, and a small number of others stayed to protect Tim and the others.

"I sense evil," Peter told them all. "I'm sure it's them."

"Oh, shit. We gotta get outta here fast, y'all! Like *real fast!*" Marcus exclaimed.

"You don't gotta tell me twice," Olivia said. "I'm way ahead of you, dude."

Hastily, they all packed up a few necessities, but before they could leave, there was a loud, ominous knocking on the door. Everyone froze until they heard a booming voice say, "It's me, the chief! You all have to go now! The ones pursuing you have arrived!"

Peter flung the door open. "I know; we're ready to leave."

They followed one after another behind Chief Masaka out of the cabin. "We have some men protecting the outside of the village," he said. "We will try to buy you time to get over to the island and get the sacred items to their rightful place. Evil cannot follow, for the sacred souls of our past will protect these relics. Nonetheless, we must hurry to the river."

As they made their way to the water, it suddenly dawned

on Peter that Mahay had followed them. Shocked, Peter was prompted to ask, "Shouldn't you be with the women and children under protection, too?"

Chief Masaka and the others exchanged a look, all of them grinning smugly. "My daughter can handle herself, don't worry," he said. This brought a smile to Mahay's face for a quick second, but then she was back to being serious until they finally reached the river.

When they arrived at the water's edge, they found several canoes already prepared for them. As they prepared themselves to leave with the boats, at the edge of the village the first battle was already underway.

As the warriors lay in wait, a fog descended upon them. Their weapons were drawn, prepared for battle, but the fog had become so thick it obscured their vision. Despite this, Coakley said, "Be ready."

There were thirty of them in all, each one tense and perfectly ready for the battle to come. They were as ready as humanly possible; unfortunately, today they were not dealing with humans, but the supernatural.

Everything was quiet. Every movement made could be heard in the silence, so when a faint rustling began, the warriors knew it was time to strike. The pitter-patter of feet running through the dried, crackling leaves alerted the warriors, but they could not see their target. The anticipation was making their hearts race, when suddenly a ram charged out of the fog and hit one of the warriors so hard, he was knocked back six feet and into two other men. Charging after the ram was a flock of ravens, each one dive-bombing into another warrior as they flew past. Behind them came Justin and the rest of his crew.

The fog began to subside as the fight raged on. It was no longer needed: as valiantly as the warriors fought, they were only able to use mortal power, and they were outmatched by the vessels of ancient magic and shape-shifters. Before long, Justin and his people had forced their way past the guard and into the village. He heard another horn being blown behind him; apparently another message to whoever still remained: they had been defeated by the intruders.

The chief and the others heard the horn as well, and the kids and professor were rushed into the boats. "You will find three paths once you reach the island. Take the one that leads you westward. Once you're on the west side of the mountain, there are caves you will need to climb up to. The sun will tell you which one you must enter to fulfill your quest," the chief said. These were his last words before they would depart. "Good luck. We will do whatever we must to aid you here. Now go!"

With those final words, Chief Masaka, Mahay, Woodo, and the few others that had accompanied them shoved the canoe off the shore. They were finally on their way.

As they sailed, Peter pulled the necklace out from underneath his shirt and looked back toward Mahay. He held it tightly in his palm and nodded at her solemnly. She returned the gesture and waved goodbye to him, a sad smile on her face. She turned to her father then, who had seen the look between the two. He knew now that there was a bond between his daughter and the young aspiring shaman. He smiled at her in understanding and put a hand on her shoulder. "We must go now."

The remaining tribespeople turned and walked away from the water's edge, ready to offer the last line of defence against Justin and his gang.

Justin and his men tore through the village, ransacking many homes in the desperate search for the staff. Countless broken windows and smashed-in doors were left in their wake before Justin and his companions slowed their assault. Every inch had been uncovered, but there was no sign of anyone. When he thought this over, Justin scowled in realization: Tim and his friends weren't hiding in the village. That meant that they had already left to try and reach their destination.

"To the water!" he shouted to his warriors. Though ten had been lost on Justin's side, the morale of those who remained was still perfectly intact. They gathered quickly and headed toward the shore Tim and his friends had departed from.

Waiting for them there was the village chief, standing strong his with daughter on one side, Woodo on the other, and his warriors in a line behind them.

"Get out of our way!" Justin shouted. "You know what

we're here for! You can't hide them from us!"

"Make us," Chief Masaka replied calmly. "That's the only way you'll be able to get past us."

"I tire of this," Justin said. "Orenda, move them now!"

"Gladly." Orenda smiled devilishly as her body began to dissipate and become fog. The fog quickly rushed toward its opponent, only to hit an invisible barrier. As soon as her movements were forced to end, Orenda returned to her human form and fell backward. Outraged and baffled, Justin looked to the ground to find a magic powder had been spread in front of the People on the Water.

"I see you have a shaman in your midst," he said.

"Your evil cannot cross!" Woodo responded. He pulled out a pouch and poured the powder inside it onto his hand, then blew it on Orenda. Her body glowed for a few seconds, and when it had stopped, she scurried backward on her hands.

"What the hell did you do to me?!" she cried, standing up. She spread her arms and tried to turn back into her smoky form, but nothing happened. Her body remained solid.

"Fascinating," said a very intrigued Justin. Behind him, Raven's body transformed once more into the flock of birds he used to attack, and they, too, charged toward the barrier, only to smack against it and fall, turning back into his human form as well. He was faster than Orenda, however, and quickly stood up to run back so that he wouldn't be cursed the same way his companion had been.

"I'm impressed," Justin said, "But I know a thing or two about magic as well." He laughed and sat down, crossing his legs in the Indian style. His arms were bent, palms facing him. Justin closed his eyes and began to chant. When he opened his eyes again, they were pure black. He continued chanting, and while the words poured out of his mouth, black spots began to form in the air around everyone. At first there were only a few, then what appeared to be thousands of them began attacking the shaman's invisible barrier.

"What is this?" asked Chief Masaka.

"Dark magic," the shaman answered. "I can sense it's very powerful in him. It's weakening the barrier, so be prepared to strike."

The black mass subsided moments later, and when it was gone, the chief turned to his people. "Now!" he shouted, and led the charge to Justin and his crew. The battle had begun.

What Justin had initially thought would be an easy battle turned out to be much more difficult than he could have imagined, especially with the shaman and Mahay in tow. The People on the Water all fought with great skill and cunning. The shaman's heart and mastery of magic helped him to take out many of Justin's warriors. Once they had been knocked out, Raven had transformed into a massive cacophonous flock of birds and attacked the shaman, only to be magically redirected to slam into trees, one by one, until they had all fallen to the ground.

Meanwhile, Orenda and Mahay faced off against each other. Without her powers, Orenda was forced to fight with only her mortal strength, but this didn't seem to bother her much. "I love a good catfight from time to time," she said, then lunged at Mahay in an attempt to tackle her. Mahay quickly stepped aside and extended her arm, catching Orenda around the neck and flipping her over to land hard on her back.

"Cat fight? More like the tortoise and the hare, don't you think?" Mahay remarked. Her smugness only served to infuriate Orenda more, prompting her to get up and charge again. Once again, Mahay caught her, this time around her torso. She used her body weight to throw the witch to the ground again. She took up a defensive stance as Orenda shakily got back to her feet.

"Is that all you've got?" Mahay taunted.

"You bitch!" screamed Orenda. She ran to Mahay again and swung at her, blinded with rage, but Mahay just ducked and hit her in the stomach. Then, with an open palm, she smacked Orenda in the face, drawing blood from her nose.

"Augh!" Orenda cried, clutching her nose and falling to her knees. She was clearly no match for Mahay in her mortal form, but she got up and rushed Mahay anyway, catching her off-guard and knocking her to the ground. Orenda quickly straddled Mahay and struck her across the face. Enraged, she grabbed a rock just off to the side and raised it above her head.

"Eat this, bitch!" Orenda shouted. She brought the stone down quickly, attempting to club the other woman's head, but Mahay, thinking quickly, grabbed a fistful of dirt and threw it in Orenda's face. Orenda flinched, momentarily blinded, and that was all Mahay needed to throw the witch off her and roll out of the way. Orenda landed face-first in the soil, then, like a fox, Mahay jumped on her back and wrapped her hands around her foe's neck, choking her until she passed out.

With everyone else otherwise occupied, Justin and Chief Masaka were left to face each other. Justin had changed himself into a massive grizzly bear, lunging at his enemy with wide, sharp claws. The chief had to roll out of the way of the assault, underneath the bear and around to his back. Once he was behind Justin, he hit the bear over the head with a large broken branch he'd found on the ground nearby. Justin roared in agony, then changed back into his normal form. Realizing that Tim and the others were slowly but surely getting away, he knew that this fight had to end quickly. He couldn't just leave, however, so he calmed himself down to settle into a sort of trance. He began to move about, almost dancing, as words began spilling from his lips in another chant. As he danced, the sky began to darken.

"Father, what's he doing?" Mahay asked her father.

Although the chief was embroiled in a fight with one of Justin's men, he turned his head in his daughter's direction. "I'm not sure, but it looks like some sort of rain dance!"

"Yes," Woodo confirmed. "He's summoning a storm." As

he spoke, drops of rain began falling hard, and thunder boomed intensely. Soon everyone was drenched. But Justin, pleased with the rain, looked up to the sky and raised a hand, screaming, *"Oh do ma ha donka!"*

A stream of lightning tore through the sky and stopped in his outstretched hand, then surged through his body. Grinning maniacally, Justin turned to face the chief and extended his other hand.

"Run!" Woodo yelled, knowing what would come next. They didn't get far before lightning came shooting out of Justin's hand, hitting all of them and knocking them unconscious. Nearby, Orenda was roused by the rain. Noticing that everyone was unconscious, she crawled over to one of the fallen warriors to take a knife from his corpse. She loomed over Mahay's body, knife poised over the girl's heart.

"Let's make sure they're dead," she hissed.

"We don't have time!" Justin snapped. "The others are our priority; these idiots are only roadblocks. We must get the staff before it's too late!" Once again, he turned his gaze skyward and shouted the same chant at the clouds as before. By his command, the storm ceased, and he began running to the water's edge, only to find that when they got there, Tim and the others had nearly reached the Island of the Ancients.

"Hurry up and get to those canoes!" Justin yelled to his crew. "I will have that staff!"

His voice echoed across the water to reach the ears of Tim and his friends. They all turned to look back at the shore, and could now see other boats pursuing them. There was enough distance between them and Justin, however, that none of the kids were worried. Feeling confident about this, Marcus stood up in the middle of the canoe and flashed his middle finger at the pursuers. This infuriated Justin. "Fuck *me*?" he yelled. "No, fuck *you*!" With a loud cry, he took a running start toward the water and dove straight in.

"Yeah, good luck!" Marcus yelled after him.

"Why are you antagonizing him?" Tim snapped.

"Marcus, you mustn't stir the pot," Peter added. "We need to stay focused on the mission and not make more trouble for ourselves!"

"Damn," Marcus said, sitting back down and crossing his arms. "Y'all act like that fool gonna catch up to us. He ain't no damn Aquaman!" He shook his head and then pointed to the island a few feet away. "Plus, we're almost there."

Everyone murmured in agreement. It was silent for nearly five minutes before Olivia looked over the edge of the boat. "Damn, I don't think he's come up for air yet! Can anybody see him?" she asked.

"Nope," replied Tim. "So either he really is Aquaman, or he's drowned."

Another few silent moments passed, but then all of a sudden there was a visible ripple in the water, and it was headed straight toward them. Professor Waters was the first to notice it. "What the hell is that?" he asked, pointing to the uneven water.

"I don't know, but it can't be good," Peter said. "Brace yourselves, everyone!"

Just as the words left his mouth, out of the water jumped a killer whale. "Oh, shit!" yelled Tim.

"Everyone, out of the canoe!" Peter instructed. Everyone did as they were told but Olivia, who had thrown herself to her knees on the boat and began praying. Marcus looked up from the water to see her and hauled himself back up the side of the canoe to pull her in with him. He had grabbed her just in time, as the moment she hit the water, the whale had smashed the boat to pieces. The waves it caused forced everyone under the water for a few seconds.

One by one, everyone's heads popped back up out of the water. "Is everyone all right?" Professor Waters called out.

"Yes," everyone called back. A few seconds later, Olivia shouted, "Wait, where's Tim? Oh my God!"

As soon as he realized that a member of their party was missing, Peter dove under the water to see the orca dragging Tim down by the foot, trying to drown him. Peter swam to the whale pulled out a knife, sinking it into the orca's flesh near the fin. He stabbed repeatedly until the whale let Tim go. By now, the others had come down to help as well. Marcus and Olivia dove to grab the unconscious Tim and help carry him up to the surface. Thankfully, they were close to the land by this time and were able to pull Tim up onto the island's shore. Once he was laid flat on the sand, the professor began to give Tim mouth-to-mouth to try and return him to consciousness. Before long, Tim was coughing up water. "Thank God," said Professor Waters. He then turned to the others. "Look after him; I'm going back for Peter."

"But Peter's right there," Olivia said, pointing just off the shore where the shaman had resurfaced only seconds ago. He made his way to the others slowly and breathlessly, practically dragging himself out of the water. He flopped down to the ground, panting heavily.

"Tim, are you okay?" he asked. Tim was now leaning on some rocks, also trying to catch his breath.

"Yeah," he said. "And I have you to thank for that. Thanks for saving my life."

"No worries. I'm just glad you're okay."

"We all are," Olivia said. "I think this calls for a group hug." Everyone smiled, and the group shared a long, heartfelt embrace.

When they pulled apart, Professor Waters looked directly at Marcus. "No more taunting. Agreed?"

"Agreed."

"Good. Now I hate to break up the love fest, but we still have a job to do, and I don't see those guys turning back," the professor said. Everyone turned to look and stood up, ready to move on with their quest.

Marcus paused for a minute. "So this is the famous Island of the Ancients, the place we've been fighting for days to get to? Hell, ain't nothing really special about this place! It looks just like everything else we've seen!"

Peter gave Marcus a wry grin. "Maybe we should see more of the island before you come to any final conclusions," he said.

"Yeah, true dat," Marcus agreed. Olivia just rolled her eyes and shook her head at his assumptions.

As they continued to walk, Tim and Peter struck up a conversation. "Do you think that killer whale was Justin?" Tim asked.

"Yes, I do," Peter responded.

"Do you think he's dead?" Olivia jumped in.

"I don't know. I managed to stab him a few times, but I can't tell for sure. I don't think he would give up quite so easily, though."

Meanwhile, there was another ripple in the water, this time headed straight for the boat that Orenda and Raven were sitting in. From the ripple, Justin appeared and pulled himself out of the water and into the boat. He was bleeding heavily from the arm.

"What the hell happened to you?" Orenda asked.

"Never mind me, they got away. Raven, fly above and keep an eye on them so we know where they are," Justin said.

"No problem." His body began to change again, this time to the form of a single raven, and he flew off.

"You gonna be okay?" Orenda asked once Raven had left.

"I'll be fine."

Tim and his friends were following the trail Chief Masaka had detailed to them when Raven came across the group, descending upon them unseen. He hid in a tree overlooking the trail, which was mostly made up of twigs and thick brush.

"Man, we need a machete or something!" Marcus whined. "These branches all keep smacking me in the face."

"Hey, looks like a clearing up ahead!" Tim shouted, ignoring Marcus's complaints. The small group walked through the clearing to find the most beautiful old redwood trees surrounding them as far as the eye could see. Everyone stopped briefly to take it all in.

"Wow, this is beautiful," Olivia said.

"Yeah, it really is, my young friend," Professor Waters agreed. After a few more minutes, they continued to follow the trail until eventually running into one of several totem poles scattered amongst the redwoods. Professor Waters took particular interest in this finding: as soon as he saw the first one, his eyes lit up like a child's on Christmas Day.

"Oh my, these are beautiful," he said. He moved in close to investigate the poles, trying to discern what each carving represented. "Don't you agree, Peter?"

There was no response. "Peter?" Professor Waters called again, but there was still no answer. Peter just remained still where he stood, eyes unfocused and staring straight ahead of him. Concerned, the kids began to turn their attention on the young shaman.

"You okay?" asked Marcus. Peter didn't answer.

"This is real creepy," Olivia mumbled as she waved her hand in front of Peter's unblinking eyes to try and get his attention. But suddenly her attention was snapped away from him when the sound of naive drums reached her ears.

"Sounds like things just got creepier," Tim whispered. He and the others began looking around frantically, trying to find the source of the noise. The drumming continued for a few minutes before abruptly stopping. As soon as it did, Peter took in a deep, shaky breath and stumbled backward.

"I could hear them," he croaked. "I could hear them and feel their presence all around me. I could feel their energy. It was so... refreshing."

"I can see why spirits would want to roam here, I guess," Marcus said with a shrug. "It's a pretty nice place."

Tim sighed. "I just want to get this stuff back so we don't have to deal with stuff like that anymore. So things can get back to normal."

"Yeah, true," Olivia agreed.

"Man," Marcus said. "It sucks that we ain't getting paid for this stuff."

"Marcus, you're getting paid with gratitude!" Peter said. "By doing this, you're saving mankind, my friend."

"So I guess you're saying this is more important than getting paid in actual money?"

"Yes, exactly."

"Gotcha."

Tim rolled his eyes before jumping into the conversation, saying, "Who cares about money if you won't live to spend it?"

"True that," Olivia agreed.

As they chattered amongst themselves, the time seemed to fly by. An hour had barely registered by the time they got to the west side of the mountain. Once they were there, Professor Waters was the first one to notice the entrances to three caves the chief had told them about, all in close proximity to one another. They seemed to be nearly 40 feet up. "I believe we've found what we were looking for, friends. Look up there," he said, pointing near the top of the cliff.

"You're close to us now," a voice hissed in Tim's ear.

Tim's eyes darted back and forth, trying to find who had whispered to him, but he saw nothing. He opened his mouth to ask if anyone else had heard it, but he didn't want to worry anyone. He decided to keep the voice he'd heard to himself.

"Damn," Marcus said, "We gotta go all the way up there?"

"Yes, we have to climb up. Unless you want to make like a bird and fly up ahead of us," Tim replied.

"Man, you know I don't know how to turn this thing on and off. It only happened that one time in the woods, the first time we ran into Justin."

"Well then, stop complaining and start climbing."

Everyone moved up to the rock face and tried to find good holds to pull themselves up on. Soon they were off the ground, heading toward the caves. About ten minutes into the climb, however, a voice suddenly called out, "You mind if we join the party?"

Marcus was the first to turn around to see Justin and his group at the bottom of the mountain. He swore loudly as a raven swooped down from the sky, taking the shape of a man as it landed next to Justin. "Good work," Justin said to him. John Raven smirked.

"No, we'll have to pass!" Professor Waters shouted.

"Oh, but I insist," Justin replied. He turned to look at Raven and his other henchmen. To head the charge, one of them, with a running start, turned himself into a ram, and

Raven became his flock. The ram was the first to run up the mountain, knocking up the professor when he reached him. Raven's flock then tried to knock off Marcus and Olivia, which they eventually did.

As they fell, Marcus and Olivia's heart rates soared, and they began to change shape as the adrenaline surging through them triggered their transformations. Soon Olivia had taken on the form of a white wolf, and Marcus that of a gigantic eagle. Marcus swooped down to catch the professor just before he hit the ground. Professor Waters looked up. "Not you again," he mumbled. In the meantime, Olivia had landed and was now tussling with the ram on the ground.

Still on the mountain, Tim and Peter watched the fight from above. Peter looked over at Tim and yelled, "Tim, no matter what, don't stop! If they get their hands on the staff, the world is doomed!"

"I understand," Tim called back. "I won't let you down!"

He began to climb again, but all of a sudden, Justin began scaling the mountain quickly, almost like a spider scurrying up a wall. Peter caught sight of him, and when Justin was almost upon them, he pulled out a tomahawk he was given by Chief Masaka as a keepsake.

"Don't stop, no matter what!" he told Tim again. His tone worried the teenager, so he looked down and saw Peter jump from the cliff, falling toward Justin and brandishing his tomahawk. Even though he was uneasy, Tim kept his word and continued to climb up the side of the mountain.

Right below him, Peter fell directly on to Justin, causing him to fall as well. As they both tumbled in the air, the two men began to fight. Just before they hit the ground, though, Justin turned himself into a grizzly to break his fall. Peter landed on the bear, thus breaking his fall, too. He ended up rolling off of the bear and tumbling a few feet. Meanwhile, Justin changed back to his human form. The two stood up, stumbling a little bit, clearly shaken from the huge fall. Undeterred, however, they began charging at each other again once they got their bearings. Justin turned himself into a bison and caught Peter off guard, slamming right into him and knocking him off his feet.

The fighting on the ground was fierce. Olivia, still in the form of a wolf, faced off with the ram, avoiding a charge from it and grabbing its hind leg with her teeth from behind, redirecting the charge into the nearby cliff to knock it unconscious. She padded over to it to make sure it was finished, and right before her, the ram changed back into its human form. It was the man that had changed into a cougar before, and he was still down for the count. Olivia then turned her attention to Orenda, who was still unable to change. Her fear was evident as she began to cautiously back up, looking side to side for an escape route. As Olivia slowly crept toward her, out of nowhere, the familiar flock of ravens dove at her full-speed. To stop them, Marcus—still holding the professor—swooped down between the flock and Olivia, swatting each bird away with his massive wings.

"Please put me down now!" Professor Waters screamed. Marcus did as he was asked and touched back down to the ground, turning back into himself. He turned to find Olivia, who had also transformed.

"Are you okay?" he asked her.

"Yeah, I'll be fine," she answered, though she was clearly rattled.

"What about you, Professor? You okay?" Marcus asked.

"Yeah... I'll be okay. Where's Peter?"

"I don't know!" Olivia called back.

"You looking for your friend?"

Marcus, Olivia, and Professor Waters all turned to see Justin smirking and holding up and banged-up Peter.

"This is bad," Marcus mumbled under his breath.

"Who you telling?" Olivia replied.

It was easy to see that the kids and professor were clearly outnumbered and on the verge of losing. But just when they seemed about to fall, a horn sounded and the survivors from the People on the Water tribe had arrived to join the fight. They were a group of nearly thirty; leading the group was Chief Masaka, Mahay, and Woodo. Though they added much strength, their arrival may have come too late. Seeing that the fighting odds were about to change, Justin pulled a knife from his pocket and held it to the unconscious Peter's neck.

"I'll slit his throat like a pig unless I get that staff!" he shouted.

"No!" Mahay shouted, furious. She started to lunge for Justin, but her father held her back.

"Do you hear me up there, Tim? I will kill him!" Justin shouted. He could feel Peter stirring in his arms, and tightened his grip, but Peter had woken up.

"Don't do it, Tim! Keep going or he'll kill us all!" the shaman cried out, though his voice was hoarse.

"Shut up!" Justin snapped.

From where he was on the cliff, Tim could hear the frenzied noises of the battle below. He had finally reached the entrance to the right cave, but just before he went in, he could hear a voice calling out to him: Justin. "You enter that cave and your friend won't live to see you come out!" Tim's friends were still yelling at him to ignore Justin and just go inside, but Tim was conflicted. He stopped just outside the entrance and closed his eyes, thinking about his friends and his time with them. He thought about what they meant to him and what they had gone through to help him.

He opened his eyes. Just before him, in the entrance of the cave was the spirit of the boy from his dream. "Hello, Tim," the spectre said.

"Hello," Tim replied, a little nervously. "You're the boy from my dream, aren't you?"

"Yes, I am. My name is Moki."

"Moki?"

"Yes. I'm sure you've noticed that we can share our thoughts," he said. "The reason why is because our souls are connected through the staff."

"But why won't it work for me?" Tim asked, gazing at the object in his hand.

"It has when you've needed it the most," Moki replied. "But to unleash its awesome power, you must call for it. To do this, say *'Watobsie n arowby'* three times."

"Watobsie n arowby..." Tim repeated. "Is that all I have to do?"

"Yes, but be warned: only use it in extreme danger against evil."

Tim looked down at the staff again. "Okay. I will." He turned and looked at the entrance of the cave as he heard Justin call out to him once more.

"You have ten seconds to throw me the staff or I will kill your friends!" he yelled. Justin began counting down loudly, starting from ten, causing Tim to panic.

"Face the evil," Moki said, bringing Tim's attention back to him. "Invoke the power of the four winds and save your friends."

Tim nodded, then made his way back from the entrance of the cave and onto the outer ledge to look down at what was going on. He could see Justin and hear him counting down ("Seven... six..."), and then noticed that Orenda's body was changing again. Justin gestured for her to change forms and get into a strategic position when he noticed this. While Peter and the others were watching Tim and not paying attention, she once again became a cloud of mist and discreetly floated up in the air.

"Be ready to attack!" Justin told the rest of his crew.

Behind Tim, Moki frowned. "I, too, have been in this situation and had to face evil. A lot of good people died in the aftermath. You have seen it in your dreams. It could happen again. Tim, this is why you were led to the staff."

"I understand," replied Tim, "And I will end this today."

"I know you will. That's why we chose you."

When Tim turned around to say one last word to the spirit, it had vanished. By now, Justin's counting had reached three. Tim turned to face his foe, standing at the edge of the ridge.

"Justin, this must stop now. Release my friends and no harm will come to you or the others," Tim called out. He sounded confident and proud, something that both Justin and Tim's friends were able to pick up on. Justin snorted.

"You can't harm me, boy! Now throw me the staff, or you will all die!"

"So be it," Tim said. He took a step back and began chanting *"Watobsie n arowby, Watobsie n arowby, Watobsie n arowby..."* As he spoke, the wind began to pick up and lifted him up off his feet. His eyes went blank as he raised his arms up to the sky. Everyone watched with amazement.

Justin looked at Orenda. "Now!" he shouted to her. She rushed forward, still in mist form, trying to sneak up on Tim and attack him. In anticipation of her attack, Tim raised the staff and pulled a jet stream out of the air, catching her up in it and forcing her away and into space. He then used the winds to pick up his friends and bring them up to the ledge at the cave's entrance, leaving only Justin and the remnants of his crew on the ground.

"Your evil ends here," Tim said. Raven transformed again in response, crying out as he flew to attack Tim as well. He too got swept up, Tim wrapping him up in a small tornado. He then hurled monsoon winds at everyone on the ground but Justin, sending them skidding miles away. Justin, defiant as ever, attempted another rain dance and conjured another thunderstorm. Just like in the previous battle, he raised a hand to the sky and pointed the other one toward Tim to redirect the lightning. The lightning struck him and he channelled it through his body, then shot it out of his fingers at Tim. Tim was fast, however, and dodged. Frustrated that he couldn't hit Tim, Justin turned his attention to the others waiting on the cliff. He shot a bolt of lightning at the cliff, missing Tim's friends but hitting the rock face just above them and causing an avalanche to come crashing down toward them. Before the rocks could hit anyone, Tim caught them with a massive gale and pushed them toward Justin. Justin turned and ran away, calling back, "I will never stop fighting, do you hear me?"

From the sky, Tim looked down on him. "If you want the staff that badly, then you can have it!"

He threw the staff downwards, and it hurled toward Justin. With every turn it made in the air, the winds intensified until they had surpassed the strength of a monsoon. It hit the ground, the impact clearing every tree within the mile and causing a huge crater in the ground. Justin was forced downward by the winds, buried alive deep inside the crater.

A few moments passed where everything but the hurling winds were still, and Tim made a gesture with his hand. The staff flew back to his hand and he pointed it back at the crater. Dirt, collapsed trees and debris arose into the air and descended back to the ground, filling in the massive deep hole and sealing Justin underneath. When all was done, Tim's feet touched the ground of the mountain's ledge. He turned to look at his friends and found them all staring at him, mouths hanging wide open.

"Everyone okay?" Tim asked.

"Uh, y-yeah, I guess," Olivia stammered, still obviously stunned. "You?"

"Yeah, I guess." Tim shrugged, then collapsed on the ground. Everyone ran to help him, but he raised his hand. "I'm fine, I just need to sit down for a minute. Catch my breath, you know."

A few minutes passed before he stood up again. The shaman of the People on the Water faced him. "It's time to finish your quest."

"Damn, man," Marcus said. "Won't you let the brother get a little rest? He gotta be tired after demolishing that motherfucker."

"Yeah, he just saved our lives!" Olivia chimed in.

"It's okay," Tim said, "He's right. With all the stuff I've seen recently, I don't need any more surprises."

He put an arm around Marcus's shoulder and another around Olivia's, and they helped walk him to the cave. Chief Masaka, Woodo, Peter, and Professor Waters all followed after the three friends, lighting torches when they entered the cave. Ritualistic symbols lined the walls, more and more appearing the deeper they went into the cave. The paintings converged in the corner where a small altar made of stone sat. It was nearly identical to the one they had found the treasures on before. One by one, the three kids placed their items on the altar, starting with Tim. Once they were all laid down, the kids took a few steps back and stared. A sudden, surreal light began to appear around the altar. The lights grew to form several spirits, all dressed in traditional Native garb. They were the first to own these items, and in the forefront was Moki. Behind him was the tribe's chief that had bestowed him with the staff. His daughter floated next to him, and the kids recognized her as the witch, Farrah. Beside her was the shaman of the tribe.

"You have all done well," the old chief said. "We want to thank you for finishing our quest. This is where we were headed before we ran into trouble. We made our last stand in front of this cave and created a cloaking spell that would not only mask the items from evil, but protect them. The reason we brought you here is because you are pure of heart, Tim, and so are your friends. We did not want evil to beat you to the items. We knew you would make it."

Farrah's spirit then glided forward, smiling. "Thank you for helping me to find my way back to my family, where I belong."

Tim nodded. "Thank you for your sacrifice," he said. "We couldn't have done this without your help." Farrah smiled again and nodded her head, then stepped back to allow Moki to step forward.

"Tim, we will always be brothers through the staff now. Never forget me or the bond we share. I hope you have a safe journey home," he said. The four ghosts then vanished along with the items left on the altar, leaving Tim and his friends to make their way back to the village.

EPILOGUE

Finally, everyone had arrived back at the village. After tending to the injured party members, they put on a celebration for their final night in the village and for finishing their long, arduous quest. They danced, told stories, and drank—at least, the adults did.

"Thank you for your bravery," Chief Masaka said to the kids, Peter, and Professor Waters in front of the entire village just before the festivities came to a close. "We consider all of you honorary members of our tribe. We will tell your story for years to come, so that our people will never forget you."

"Thank you," the group of five replied. All of them smiled, the tears in their eyes threatening to fall.

"And with that, I think it's time we called it a night," Chief Masaka announced. "Once again, we thank you."

With that, everyone turned in for the night and returned to their cabin, with the sole exception of Peter. He was restless and knew he wouldn't be able to sleep, so he took a stroll to the lake. He sat down by the water's edge and silently enjoyed the breeze and peace. Then, suddenly, he heard a rustle coming from the bush behind him. Not taking any chances, he jumped up into a defensive stance. From the leaves appeared Mahay.

"Sorry," she said, "I didn't mean to scare you."

"That's okay," Peter replied. "With all the excitement today, I guess I just can't help but be cautious."

"I understand." She stepped closer to him. "So, you mind if I join you?"

"Sure."

Mahay sat down next to him. It was a beautiful night out, and the full moon reflected off the water perfectly, the image almost unmoving. "Do you think you'll miss it here?" she asked.

"I'm sure I will."

"What will you miss the most?"

"If I'm honest..." Peter took a deep breath and turned to face her, looking Mahay directly in the eye. "You."

Surprised and blushing, Mahay replied, "Oh, really? Why will you miss me?"

"Because you're everything I look for in a woman. You're strong, gentle, sweet, beautiful..." he would have continued, but before he could, she had leaned in and kissed him.

"I like you, too," she said, pulling away. Peter smiled and leaned in again, kissing her back. She wrapped her arms around his neck, and he pulled himself a little closer to her. Unbeknownst to the two, however, Chief Masaka watched from a distance. He didn't stay long, choosing to walk away without a word.

They pulled away from each other and laughed quietly.

The rest of the time they spent together was uneventful; Mahay leaned her head on Peter's shoulder and they gazed out onto the lake together.

Bright and early the next morning, Tim and the others woke up and began to pack their things for the long trip home. The People on the Water loaded them up with meat and fruit for the journey, and gave gifts of necklaces, wrist bands, and similar trinkets. They symbolized warriors, and the gifts from the tribe's shaman were supposed to ward off evil spirits.

"Mahay will help guide you, if you'll have her," Chief Masaka offered.

Everyone nodded; Peter especially was happy about having her come along. After that, they all said their goodbyes quickly, not wanting to drag out the sad affair, and headed home.

"You are one of us now and will always be welcomed here," said Chief Masaka as they started walking away. "Have a safe journey, friends."

It took them a few days, but the small group finally found themselves back where their journey began. In those few days, everyone could tell that Peter and Mahay had become closer. As they loaded their things into the truck to go home, it dawned on the professor that Mahay would have to find her way home by herself. "Mahay, would you be all right going back to your village on your own?" he asked, but before she could answer, Peter stepped in front of her.

"Well," he began, almost sheepishly, "She won't be going back alone. I'm going with her. If she'll have me, that is."

"Well yes," Mahay said, stunned. "But are you sure you want to give up the life that you know for my tribe's way of life?"

"All my life I've been searching for something, but I did not know what that something was. I've found it being with your people and being with you. I believe this is my path," Peter replied. Mahay smiled and embraced Peter happily, kissing him on the lips.

"I knew it! I *knew* something was up between you two!" Olivia squealed.

"You're a lucky man, bro," Marcus added. "I'm happy for you."

"So am I," said Tim. "I wish you both much happiness."

"Thank you," Peter and Mahay said together. They smiled and shook everyone's hands.

"All right everyone," Professor Waters said, "Let's get going. Real life awaits us."

"Wait." Before they all got in the car to drive off, Peter put a hand on Professor Waters' shoulder. "Would you mind giving me a lift back to my village so I can speak with the chief?"

"Sure." He nodded and opened the door so everyone could climb in the truck.

The ride home was mostly silent, as everyone was reflecting on their adventures and what had led them up to this point. The first stop was the reservation Peter was from, then Tim's house, then Marcus, Olivia, and finally Professor Waters. Once alone, he leaned his seat back and exhaled. "How did one look at eBay lead to all of this?" he mumbled to himself, then he burst into uncontrollable laughter as he drove home.

When Tim got home, his mother and father were waiting for him. He rushed forward to hug them and exchanged warm greetings. "We have a surprise for you," his father said, and he stepped aside to reveal Josette waiting for him. She came out of the kitchen with roses in her hands.

"I missed you!" Josette exclaimed, hugging him tightly.

"I missed you more," Tim replied. He took the flowers and laughed. "You know, the only thing more beautiful than these flowers is the person who delivered them."

"Aww, you're so sweet." Josette giggled and gave Tim and even bigger hug. As they embraced, Tim's parents left the room, deciding it was time to leave them alone.

Marcus walked in the door to his house, and the first thing he did was pick up the phone and dial Fatima's number. "Hey babe," he greeted when she picked up.

"Hi Marcus!" Fatima answered excitedly. It was easy to tell that she had been eager to hear from him. "How was your trip?"

"Very adventurous. I'll never forget it."

Later that night, Olivia was sitting on her back porch, strumming her guitar and watching the stars. She was in a reflective mood, still asking herself if that whole adventure had actually happened. She had exchanged happy greetings with her parents before coming out here. It felt good to be home, but at the same time, she almost missed the journey.

A few days later, life had returned to normal. Peter and Mahay, after spending some quality time with Peter's family, had returned to Mahay's village, Professor Waters was preparing for the start of school, and Tim, Marcus, Olivia, Josette and Fatima all met up for ice cream for the last time before they went off to college.

"So I guess this is the last day before everything changes," Tim said.

"Yup," Olivia replied.

"Hey," Marcus chimed in, "We had to grow up sometime."

"True, but I'll miss days like this, hanging out with you guys," Olivia said.

"Hey, let's make a pact," Tim said, extending his spoon. "Around this time every year, we'll all meet up here for dessert. All in favor, join spoons."

Everyone put their spoons on top of Tim's, joining them together. The pact was made and everyone smiled. There they were: five friends, each of them ending one journey and beginning another.